DO NOT REMOVE
CARDS FROM POCKET

ALLEN COUNTY PUBLIC LIBRARY
FORT WAYNE, INDIANA 46802

You may return this book to any agency, branch,
or bookmobile of the Allen County Public Library.

DEMCO

WESTERN VENGEANCE

WESTERN
VENGEANCE

•

DON HEPLER

AVALON BOOKS
THOMAS BOUREGY AND COMPANY, INC.
401 LAFAYETTE STREET
NEW YORK, NEW YORK 10003

PRINTED IN THE UNITED STATES OF AMERICA
ON ACID-FREE PAPER
BY HADDON CRAFTSMEN, SCRANTON, PENNSYLVANIA

WESTERN
VENGEANCE

Prologue

Watt's gun slid from his worn holster in the smooth movement he had practiced so long, the cylinder turning as his thumb reefed back on the hammer. The barrel had barely cleared the leather when he twisted it upward and dropped his wrist at the same time to bring it up just that split second quicker. He never consciously pulled the trigger, never remembered pulling the trigger afterward, but fire and noise blasted across his open holster, and the man with the bent nose and bad teeth grunted heavily as the lead slug slammed into his belly down low. His hand was on his own gun, but the barrel had never even cleared the leather.

1

Watt thumbed back the hammer and fired again. This time the slug smashed into the man's chest, ramming him backward. Always shoot them twice. Watt had learned that the hard way. One bullet may not stop a man, but two quick shots and he was going down for sure and could not hurt you anymore.

The man backpedalled, and Watt could smell the sour breath from him where that last slug had knocked the wind from his body. It smelled of rotten teeth and bad whiskey, and the man glared into his eyes and finally lost his balance and fell onto his back on the wood floor. His fingers clawed at the wood as if trying to dig into it, and one of his fingernails peeled back and hung at a weird angle, but the man seemed not to notice and kept digging at the unyielding wood.

His expression became more and more distant, as if he were seeing things nobody else could see, and finally his movements slowed, stopped, and he was dead except for his right foot, which twitched reflexively for another few seconds.

The bar had remained absolutely still, with not another man making the tiniest movement, lest it be misconstrued as an attempt to intervene. Expressions around the room clearly indicated their surprise at the outcome of the altercation.

"Man hadn't ought to force a fight with a stranger," Watt said, not aware of how cold and hard it really sounded.

"I would say he found that out," the bartender said matter-of-factly. He set the can of peaches he had been holding in front of Watt, breaking the spell of stillness in the room. "He has done that to others before," he went on. "He could not hold his whiskey and turned mean. It was bound to catch up with him sooner or later, and you doubtless saved other lives by doing him in sooner instead of later."

Watt reloaded, a movement not lost on the others, then eased his gun back into his holster. He put a quarter on the bar for the peaches. Somehow he was no longer hungry, and he picked up the can in his left hand and turned, ready to leave. He watched as one of the other men pushed back his chair and came over to look at the dead man. He studied on him for a moment, then looked up at Watt.

"He died hard," he said. Watt looked back, eyes smoky and disturbing.

"Men always die hard," he said softly. "Every living thing dies hard," and he walked out.

Chapter One

Sunset, huge and red, the beginning of the end of day three. Despair had set in rock hard, pressing down on the girl/woman, rounding her young shoulders, dulling her senses. That was why she didn't see him at first.

Her thoughts were of water, any water. Cool water would be best, maybe flowing up from underground in a small bubbling spring like they had found so many days ago. Cool and clear and soft and smooth on the throat, it would wet her parched insides. She could almost feel her dry tissues soak up the life-giving fluid; could almost feel the soft smoothness as she took swallow after swallow of the cool, wet stuff. Almost.

5

But it was not to be, for she had found no water and the sun was going down and it was the end of day three. Somehow she knew there would be no end to day four.

Her once pretty blue dress hung in tatters where Alvin had tried to rip it from her, and she was sorry it was ruined, but guessed it wouldn't matter much in the long run. She hoped he was suffering as much as she was. She hoped he was dying in agony and knew it was wrong to feel that way but couldn't help herself. Scalding was awful to think about, but if anyone deserved it, he did, and gentle as she was, she couldn't find it in herself to feel sorry about doing it to him.

But she was a fighter. Her paw was a fighter with no quit in him, and no matter if she died or not, she would do him proud because she loved him. And so she plodded on. Toward the half ball that was the setting sun. Toward the west. Toward her paw.

She actually bumped into Watt, jarring to a surprised stop. Something in her recognized that she was in his shade, and she looked up where he sat astride his great horse, silhouetted against the blood-red orb. He was so big, so tall, and he looked down at her, but she couldn't see his face because of the brightness of the sun. She tried to smile, tried to speak.

He began to waver, to shimmer like waves of heat rising off the endless prairie, and she was afraid he would go away. Afraid he wasn't real, wasn't solid, so she reached up and put her hand on his thigh, feeling the solid muscle there.

Watt looked down at the woman in stunned silence as she slid to the ground beside Horse, a crumpled-up puddle of sun-burned skin and torn blue cloth. He could still feel where her small hand had touched his leg.

He had her head cradled in his arm and was patting her sunburned face real easy with his wet neckerchief when she opened her eyes. They were blue and looked old for such a young woman. He gently patted the cool cloth against her, and she looked up at him.

"Where have you been?" she asked accusingly.

Watt was surprised. He was certain he had never seen her before.

"I walked and walked," she went on, every word an effort. "Ever so far . . . ever so far. . . ." Her eyes started to droop closed once more, then snapped open and appraised him again.

"Please, be a nice man," she said.

"I will do my best, ma'am," he replied.

"I'm sorry," she said. Suddenly her face clouded up, and she began to cry, only there were no tears. "I'm sorry. I'm sorry," she kept repeating.

"There, there," he said, soft and soothing. "You'll be all right now."

"I'm sorry."

"There, there," and he patted the cool cloth against her face softly. Her eyes closed once more, and he first thought she was asleep or worse, but she sucked noisily at his canteen when he pressed it against her cracked lips, and she moaned in frustration when he took it away after only a few swallows.

He made camp, built a fire, hobbled Horse and cooked some beans and bacon. About every half hour he would offer her more water, and she would suck eagerly at it but would not wake up. He forked beans into his mouth and watched the young woman sleep. A dozen questions rolled around in his mind, but they would have to wait for answers until she had healed some.

Once finished with dinner, he gently

raised her in the crook of his arm and offered another drink. When she finished, he put a forkful of beans into her mouth and waited for a reaction. She chewed once, then again, and her eyes came open. She took all he put into her and ate like she had not eaten in days, which she hadn't.

Finished, she looked up at him, all serious and somber for a minute, then snuggled down and went back to sleep right there in his arm. He sat there motionless for a long time, looking down at this woman. She was plenty tough, or she wouldn't have made it as far as she had. He knew that. But she looked so childlike and peaceful lying there, he hated to disturb her until the fire finally burned down and the night cold began to creep in on them.

He picked her up, light as almost nothing at all, and laid her on his bedroll, head on his saddle. She moaned and stirred slightly, but never woke up. Then, because he couldn't think of any other way to do it, he lay down next to her and covered them both with the blanket. For a man who always slept alone, it was mighty strange to have someone breathing so close to his head, but he got used to it and gradually, gun in hand like usual, fell asleep himself.

It was just before dawn when he woke. Cold. Hard cold, with the promise of winter to come. She was snuggled up against his back, and he could feel her warmth and soft-ness against him. Somehow it didn't feel at all uncomfortable. In fact, it felt more like the way things were supposed to be. He lay there and thought about that for a long time as he listened to her steady breathing.

He watched the sunlight slide down the faraway peaks and reach across the plains toward them. It was the longest he could remember staying abed for years. Seemed like he was always having to get up early and go at it hard just to keep life in his body. Now, all of a sudden, he had to keep life in two bodies. For a little while, anyway, until he could get her back to her home.

The real strangeness of it all was that he didn't ordinarily feel alone. Seemed like he had spent so much time with himself that he had come to accept the aloneness as the way things were. But having her soft against him made the aloneness seem like it had been a bad thing all along. She moaned softly in her sleep and pulled more of the blanket from him as she rolled over back to back to him. Might as well get up as lie there without any blanket. Besides, it was sure time to get the fire going and breakfast coffee on.

He eased out and got the morning started. Because of the girl, he made the fire bigger than usual, and it was almost no time until the coffee was boiling. He poured a cup and looked across the fire at her. Her eyes were open, and she was staring at him somberly.

"Morning," he said.

"Morning," she returned.

"You feelin' any better?" he asked.

"Some," she admitted. "Cup of that coffee would help a lot."

"Surest thing," he said and gave her his cup, then poured himself another. She sat up and sipped gingerly from the metal cup, then looked across the steaming coffee at the man who had saved her life.

He was lean, with a leanness that spoke of hard times, hard living, and hard muscles. He wasn't old, but he wasn't a kid anymore, either, with a weathered face tanned by constant exposure to the outdoors. His clothes were worn but clean, and his hat had once been white but was now weathered into a nondescript gray that suited him somehow. His gunbelt had the soft patina of well-worn leather but was spotlessly clean, and he wore it with the casual comfort of an old friend. The gun butt showed plain walnut grips, and there was no sign of dirt on it, either.

"Who are you?" she asked.

"Name's Watt," he said.

"I'm Rachel," she came back. "Rachel Wagner."

"Pleased to meet you."

"I'm glad to meet you too," she said.

Watt looked across the fire at her, and the corners of his mouth turned up slightly in what passed for a smile on him.

"I believe you," he said.

He put a skillet on the fire and sliced the last of his bacon into the hot pan. It began to sizzle almost immediately, and the smell of cooking bacon wafted across the camp and reminded Rachel of days that seemed so long ago. Days when she was but a child and Mother was still alive and cooking breakfast back in Tennessee.

He sliced a baked potato into the same pan while she sipped at her coffee and watched. She sat up all the way and winced when her sunburned skin flashed hurt.

"Here," she said. "Let me do that. The least I can do is cook."

"Your sunburn won't like being close to a fire much," he said calmly. "I'll do the cookin' for right now. You just rest up. Your turn will come." It was the longest speech he had made in quite a while. He watched her from the corner of his eyes while tending to the bacon and potatoes with a fork.

She kept trying to put her torn sleeve back up on her shoulder, and it kept slipping back down. She was pretty ragged. She was pretty sunburned. She was pretty young. She was pretty.

Watt was kind of surprised at himself. He had a sister back home about her age, and he thought of her as an annoying kid. He didn't think of Rachel that way, though. He thought of her as soft and warm and pressed up against his back. The bacon spit hot grease on his hand and snapped him back to reality.

He forked half the food onto his only metal plate and handed it to her with the fork. Then he took his knife, speared a piece of fried potato, and began to eat from the skillet. They ate in silence, breaking the long fast of night with the greasy camp food of a typical range morning. Watt studied her across the fire.

She was so serious and controlled, but a few freckles scattered on each side of her nose put the lie to her mature adulthood.

Nope. Not quite yet. She was really a serious, down-to-earth woman, all grown up on the inside and just waiting for her body to catch up with her. He remembered her pressing against him. Wouldn't be too long on the body part, either.

He got a red shirt out of his saddlebag and handed it to her.

"You'd best put this on for a couple of days," he said. "Give your sunburn a chance to heal."

Rachel thought that over, then reluctantly took the shirt. It was really big for her, so she rolled the sleeves up again and again until they were at her wrists. The shirttail hung down to midthigh. It was a little scratchy on her sunburned shoulders and arms, but it would keep the sun from cooking her any further and end her struggle with modesty because of her torn dress. The shirt was clean, but it still had a faint smell, a man smell of leather and horse and yes, even of the tall man across the fire. The smell was not at all unpleasant.

"Thank you, Mr. Watt," she said.

He nodded. "I got a needle and thread if you want to fix that dress," he said.

"Maybe later," she replied. There was no

way Rachel was going to take off what was left of her dress in front of a stranger.

He shrugged. It was up to her.

"Anybody back there deserve killin'?" Watt asked. It wasn't really any of his business unless somebody was coming after her with blood in their eye, but he wanted to know. It was fairly obvious what had happened to her. Watt had been reading sign for years, and her last few days were real easy to figure out.

"I scalded him real bad," Rachel said. It wouldn't hurt to let this stranger know she could be dangerous if she had to be. "Before he could do what he had a mind to do," she added. She didn't want him to think she was a fallen woman and maybe easy prey.

"Oh." His expression didn't change, but she had just raised herself some in his estimation. She was a fighter for sure.

Rachel waited for him to ask if Alvin would be coming after them, but he didn't say anything else about that awful day.

"You heading anywhere in particular out here?" was his next question.

"Waldo," she said.

"Waldo?" He knew the town, if you could call it a town. "Not much there, ma'am.

Blacksmith, saloon, and a few scruffy miners grubbing at the mountain."

"You have been there?" she asked.

"Yes'm. Didn't stay long."

"My paw is likely one of those scruffy miners you mentioned," she said.

He had the grace to look a little embarrassed. "Come to think on it," he said, "they weren't all scruffy, exactly."

Rachel laughed. "It's all right, Mr. Watt," she said. "You can call them like you see them."

He smiled. First time he had done that, and his face lit up when he showed his white teeth.

Good looking, she was thinking. *Handsome, even. Especially when he smiled.*

Nice girl, he thought. *Sense of humor and plenty of guts. Pretty too.* He reminded himself she was little more than a child.

He broke camp, making no effort to disguise the fact they had been there. After making sure the fire was out, he saddled Horse, then turned to her.

"You ride, ma'am," he said.

It sounded mighty like an order to Rachel, but the idea of walking for another three days certainly didn't appeal to her. But she wasn't quite sure how she was going to

maintain her ladylike demeanor while riding a horse in a dress. She hesitated by the
side of the horse. He looked down at her,
and she could swear there was a twinkle
buried deep in his eyes. They stood there
for a full thirty seconds.

"Maybe if you cut a slit up the back of
your dress, you could keep your legs out of
the sun," he finally suggested.

He pulled his knife from the sheath and
handed it to her. She bent over, and the
fabric parted effortlessly in front of the
sharp blade. When she mounted, she felt an
awful draft up the back until she settled into
place, all covered proper and decent.

Watt almost had a heart attack when the
girl mounted. He could easily see the inside
of her white leg almost all the way up. It
was the firm, straight leg of a young woman,
and he knew it was something he would be
able to drag out of his memory in the coming
years and see again and again. Rachel
seemed satisfied once she was seated comfortable on Horse, so he took up the reins
and led off toward the north, allowing a big
smile to split his face once she couldn't see.

It was almost a full hour before Rachel
spoke.

"We are going north, Mr. Watt."

"Yes'm, we are," he said.

"Waldo is to the west, is it not?"

"Yes, it is," he agreed. "In about two hours we will hit hardpan, and from there it will be almost impossible for anyone to track us."

"I see." It didn't for a moment occur to her that he might not be talking about Alvin.

The desert floor gradually hardened until Horse was hardly making any tracks at all. Watt turned northeast and walked another hour, then made a sharp left and headed west. The hardpan was like rock, and Horse left no sign where they had been.

"That was very clever, Mr. Watt," she said.

"Thank you, ma'am."

They walked another hour, then stopped for a break. Rachel took the large piece of beef jerky he offered and walked about, working out the kinks after so long in the saddle. Watt fed Horse some grain and water from his hat before he took a piece of jerky for himself. He sat on a rock and rested, watching the girl stretch and walk about in his big red shirt over her torn and cut dress.

It was going to be three days out of the way to go to Waldo, but he could see no alternate plan. He obviously had to get rid of the girl, and leaving her in the desert to die never even entered his mind. Besides, he kind of liked traveling with her. He'd probably miss her some after he dropped her with her father.

Nope. No alternative. His business would just have to wait an extra week or so.

He tightened the cinch and climbed aboard, then held down a hand to Rachel. She put her foot in the stirrup, took his hand, and swung aboard behind him. Horse shuffled a couple of times as he adjusted to the new weight, then headed out, nose to the west.

About an hour before sundown, four riders tracked them onto the hardpan and reined in.

"I don't get it," Rubin said. "How come he came up on the hardpan?"

"Don't know," James answered. "Could be he knows we're followin' him."

"Don't seem likely," Wyatt said. "After all this time, seems like he'd figure we'd have given up."

The fourth man rode ahead a ways, then came back. "He turned northeast up there a piece," he said. "Tracks are hard to read, but you can see them. He's still walkin'. Girl is riding."

The men didn't doubt Greg at all. He had proved his tracking skill too many times.

"Well," Rubin said, "let's go. We can make another mile or so before dark." He made to leave.

"Hold on," Greg said. "I got a bad feeling about this."

"How so?" James asked.

"Seems like they could'a made maybe one more mile due north on the hardpan, then turned any way he wanted and we could not have tracked him at all."

"So you think he wants us to follow him?" Rubin questioned.

"Might be," Greg admitted.

"Ambush?" Wyatt asked.

The four men sat and pondered on that for a minute. You could see the idea didn't set well with any of them.

"Could be," Greg said, finally breaking the silence. "Could be he just wants us to head off in that direction while he doubles back."

Another silence.

"Sometimes I hate this business," Wyatt said, and they all chuckled.

Greg swung his horse over and headed for a jumble of rocks. The rest followed.

"Good a place to camp as any," he said back over his shoulder.

Rubin kicked his horse into motion. "What I want to know is, who's the girl?" he asked. Nobody had any answer.

Seven miles to the south, a wagon sat, tongue stabbed into the sand. The oxen were already finished with their food and grubbing about for more. Dinner cooked over the small fire, tended by a short man comically bowlegged.

"Hurry up!" a man's voice called from the wagon. Impatient. Angry.

"Hold your horses," the short man called back, then began mumbling to himself.

"I can hear you, Joel," the man in the wagon called out.

"So you can hear me," Joel said. He was tired and cranky. He didn't like having to do all the work. He finally poured a cup of coffee and took it over to the wagon.

Alvin was lying in a sitting-up position. He was covered with blankets, and still he shivered. His face was wrapped in a cut-up flour sack that stuck to the lard Joel had spread over his horrible burns. The agony was intense and unending.

He put down the haft of his whip and took the coffee. "Thanks," he gritted through the slit in the flour sack.

He tried to sip from the cup, but the hot metal brought back the fire to his lips and tears to his eyes. He forced himself to endure the pain. He wouldn't give in. He wouldn't give up. He wouldn't close his eyes and die even though that was what he wanted to do more than anything. Almost. He touched his whip once more. There was one thing he wanted to do more than die. Something worth enduring the pain for. Something that would make it all worthwhile.

Joel saw the look of hate and recognized it for what it was. In a way, he didn't blame Alvin for his hatred. No doubt about it, Alvin would spend the rest of his life as a monster, with the kind of disfigured face that would make kids blanch and adults gasp.

Joel knew all too well how people reacted to deformity in their fellow man. Being short was bad enough. His deformed legs were almost too much to bear. He knew the laughter of the kids and the whispered asides of their parents. He should be feeling sorry for Alvin. Instead, he felt a gloating pleasure at seeing someone who was once so much better looking than him being dropped to a level lower than his.

Joel thought Alvin would be better off dead, but he knew the burning anger, the drive for revenge would probably keep him alive. Too bad. She was a nice enough girl.

He went back to the fire and dinner. It was his plan to bed down early. Alvin would want to get an early start in the morning, and Waldo was still two days away.

The smell of cool from the mountains slid easy down the slopes and out to their camp in the foothills. The quiet sound of the fire was veiled by the muted splashing of a stream just below the camp. Darkness was already settling in as birds hopped around just outside the camp and sang their final chorus before night set in hard.

Watt had gone back to his usual small fire, and a rabbit was slowly cooking on a spit while the usual beans simmered in the skillet. Too bad the bacon was all gone.

The girl came back from the bushes and studiously avoided looking at him.

"How is your sunburn?" he asked.

"It will be all right."

"Coffee is ready if you want some now."

"I'll wait for you," she came back. For some reason he liked that answer.

"Getting cool, isn't it?" she asked.

"Going to freeze tonight, I'm thinking," Watt said.

"Boil all day and freeze all night," was her comment.

He thought that over. "Hard land for hard people," he said. She looked at him across the fire.

"I don't want to be a hard person," she said.

"Too bad," he came back, "On account of you already are."

She looked surprised.

"You survived out here for three days by your own self," he explained. "Then you rode with me all day and never once complained about your sunburn or how uncomfortable you were. You're fit for this land, and it's nothing to be ashamed of neither."

Rachel could think of nothing to say to that, and so, being a practical girl, she said nothing. She was pleased, however, that Watt seemed to think she was at least worthwhile. She was somewhat surprised that she valued the opinion of this man whom she had not even known a single day previously.

He handed her a plate with half the beans and a couple of choice pieces of the crispy rabbit. Rachel took the fork and dug in with gusto. She was starved and still trying to make up for her unintentional three-day fast.

Watt chewed on a piece of rabbit and watched her work on the food. Even though she was obviously ravenous, she still ate proper, taking time to finish one bite before taking another. There was nothing real ladylike about the size of the bites, however, and she forked in big mouthfuls at a time. It pleased him that he could keep her alive and fed and safe, but for the life of him he couldn't say why.

Rachel finished the rest of the rabbit and wasn't the least bit sorry to see that Watt had another one cooking already. She finished up the beans on her plate while they watched the small fire crisp up the scrawny carcass.

Watt handed her the cup of coffee. "Feeling better?" he asked.

Rachel smiled at him. "For a while there I thought I would never get full again," she said. "Sorry I ate so much of your food."

"Don't worry about that. There's more than enough for us both," he said, even though it wasn't quite true, at least not if she didn't fill up pretty soon. Oh, well, he could always fill up with jerky. Wouldn't be the first time. He sprinkled some salt on the rabbit. "Help yourself," he said and handed her his knife. He poured himself some coffee in his only other cup.

"How far to Waldo?" she asked between bites.

"Be there late day after tomorrow if nothin' happens."

"What could happen?"

"Just an expression," he assured her. She was thinking of Alvin. He wasn't.

Didn't seem likely Rubin could catch up with them before they got to Waldo, especially if he fell for that false trail on the hardpan. Long as Watt didn't hang around Waldo too long, Rubin would miss him again and get nothing for his trouble but another week of tired from following him. Rubin sure was a persistent cuss, and in a way Watt had to admire him for that. He cleaned off the few remaining pieces of rabbit while Rachel sipped her coffee.

"Got a surprise," he announced.

She raised an eyebrow and watched while he dug a can out of the saddlebag.

"Peaches!" she said, and she clapped her hands and actually giggled. It was the first time she had ever done anything childlike, and it took him back some.

"Yup. Been saving them for a while," he explained as he took his knife and opened the can. "Thought maybe tonight would be a good time to eat them." He handed the can across the fire; she forked out half a peach and nibbled at it slowly.

"Oh, this is delicious," and she sounded all grown-up again.

"Eat up and enjoy," he said. "There are eight in that can, and I never liked more than two for myself. Don't care for the syrup much, neither." He was getting too good at this lying business. If he didn't stop it pretty soon, he would likely starve to death.

She took him at his word, and when six of the golden slices were gone, she handed the can back across the fire. The two slices for him hardly seemed to satisfy his sweet tooth at all, but he nevertheless handed her the can and watched as she drank the sweet syrup down to the last drop.

"I am stuffed to the top," she exclaimed.

"I thank you sincerely, Mr. Watt. I'm a lucky girl to have a savior like you."

"Don't mention it, Rachel. It's just what anybody would have done out here. Besides, it's kind of nice to have company for a change." It was the first time he had ever said her name, and he didn't even notice that he did.

"Where am I to sleep, Mr. Watt?"

"It's my intention to bury the fire and lay the bedroll over it," he explained.

She was confused. "But where am I to sleep, Mr. Watt?"

"In the bedroll, ma'am," he explained.

"I wouldn't feel right, taking your bed," she said.

Watt looked across the fire at her. "Well, you won't be, exactly," he said.

"I don't understand."

"We'll both be sleeping in the bedroll," he said.

Rachel was stunned. "Both of us together?" she asked.

"That's correct."

"I hardly think that is proper," she said, thinking of Alvin.

"Proper or not, ma'am, it's going to freeze tonight, and that's the way it has to be," he said with a tone of finality. He cleaned the camp, scrubbing the plates with sand and rinsing them in the running stream.

Rachel tried to adjust to the idea. She was not real up-to-date on the whole man/woman thing, but Paw had seemed pretty definite about her not getting too close to any strange men. Alvin wasn't even a stranger, and look what he tried the first chance he got. Now this man, who was definitely a stranger, insisted that they actually sleep together in the same bed.

On the other hand, she could see the practicality of it. There only was one bed. It *was* going to be mighty cold. Survival itself depended on staying warm. Besides, for some reason she didn't find the idea of sleeping with Watt to be too terrifying. He wasn't like Alvin. There was something more solid and stable about him. He didn't even look at her with that weird intensity Alvin had.

She liked him. She trusted him.

Watt buried some coals from the fire deep enough so the heat would slowly rise through the night and keep the bedroll warm but not set the blankets on fire. He unrolled the bedroll and put the saddle at the head. He looked over at the shape in the dark that was the girl.

"Bedtime, Rachel," he said. It even sounded strange to him.

Rachel hesitated a moment, then moved over to the bedroll. Already the cool had turned into cold, and the promise of hard freeze bit into her exposed skin. Her legs were already cold.

She slid between the blankets, and they were already toasty and warm, driving the tense cold from her body. Watt's broad shoulders were momentarily silhouetted against the night sky as he removed his gun belt. Rachel stiffened up as he slid into the blankets behind her.

They lay there, soaking in the heat, feeling the cold night air on their exposed faces, not touching each other. It wasn't easy to avoid contact in the confining bedroll, but it could be managed.

Don't roll against him, Rachel thought. If she stayed away from him, everything would be all right. The heat soaked into her, coming from the slowly dying fire and from the man so close but so far away. He smelled of wood smoke and Horse and man. It wasn't a bad smell at all.

In spite of herself, she relaxed as the fatigue she had kept pushed back flooded over her. Watt's breathing evened out, and she lay there, forcing herself to stay alert until she figured he was asleep. Finally she relaxed all the way, allowing her eyes to close and a big sigh to escape. She was tired. So tired. Actually, it was kind of nice sleeping next to him.

"Didn't bother you any last night, neither," Watt said aloud.

Rachel opened her eyes wide and stared into the clear night sky.

Chapter Two

Rachel woke to the sound of birds fussing busily as they prepared to start their new day. She was warm, luxuriously warm, rested and comfortable. She was lying on her side, practically wrapped around the man on his back next to her. Her left arm sprawled across his chest, and her leg rested across his thighs. It felt so proper and natural, but she knew it was not proper, and her eyes popped open.

Watt lay there, eyes wide open, staring into the brightening morning sky. He had a funny expression on his face. Rachel let go of him and straightened out in the bedroll.

"Morning," she said.

He turned his head and looked at her. "Mornin'," he said back.

"I slept great," Rachel said.

"That's just wonderful," he said somewhat bitterly.

Rachel caught the tone and wondered what she had done wrong.

Watt slid out of the bedroll, put on his hat, and strapped on his gun belt. Ready for another day. He broke kindling and built a fire, not looking at her and without talking.

Rachel didn't understand why men were always so moody. Alvin had always been in a bad mood. Now Watt—Mr. Watt—seemed rather testy too. She slid out of bed and stretched life back into her sore limbs. It had been a rough few days, but her sunburn seemed a little bit better. Her skin would probably start to peel in another day or so, and that would be itchy and miserable, but it was better than being dead.

Watt handed her a cup of warmed-up coffee.

"Thank you, Mr. Watt," she said. "Please let me do the cooking now. I feel much better, and I don't care to be treated as a guest."

Watt looked at her as she poured him a coffee and held it out. He hesitated a moment, then took it with mumbled thanks.

He backed over to a handy rock and gingerly eased down.

"I am not a slacker, Rachel," he said after a sip. "I find it very difficult to sit around and do nothing while someone else is working."

She looked over at him. "Go and shoot something, then," she said. "It will probably do you good."

He grinned brightly, and suddenly the morning shined better. "You figure killing something will improve my mood, huh?" and he even laughed a little. "Sorry about being so cranky. I'm just a little tired, is all."

"I rested very well," she said as she dug out the skillet and bag of beans. "I can't imagine why you didn't."

She didn't know why he laughed at that, but he did.

"No, Rachel," he said. "I don't reckon you can."

Rubin was not in a good mood, either.

"I swear," he said, "that guy always manages to put us in rotten places to camp. I know he does it a'purpose."

James chuckled and ripped a bite from a big piece of jerky. "One minute you say he don't know we are followin' him; the next he is pickin' our campsites," he said.

"Well, stop and think on it," Rubin told him. "When was the last time we had a decent campsite? When was the last time you slept under trees with plenty of water and ground that wasn't all rocks?"

Wyatt came back into the camp. "Is Rubin whining again?" he asked. "I do believe he should have got himself another kind of work," and he laughed.

"Ain't so funny to me, neither," Greg said. "To tell the truth, I'm tired of following this guy. I think maybe he's playing with us, and I don't like it none. It's like he's not taking us serious, if you know what I mean. I ain't used to not being taken serious."

Now Rubin laughed. "When we catch him, I'll tell him he hurt your feelings."

"Darn right," Greg said with an affected pout. "That's just what he done. He hurt my feelings." They all laughed.

With practiced ease the four men broke camp and saddled up, bantering with each other as they did. It was obvious they were friends and had ridden together for a long time. They swung into the saddles and looked at Greg. He was the best tracker.

Greg shrugged. "I think we had best head

northeast and follow his trail," he said. "I 'spect he'll double back up there somewhere, only he's so sneaky sometimes, he might just keep on going in that direction."

As a single man they kicked their horses into motion and headed into the morning sun.

"You suppose that woman he found is good looking?" Rubin asked.

"Don't know," Greg answered. "She ain't real big is all I can tell from her tracks."

Rubin gave a mock sigh. "Just one more time when life has treated me real bad," he said.

"How so?" James asked.

"He gets to camp somewhere green and soft, with a beautiful woman," Rubin said and then added a loud sigh for emphasis. "I have to camp on hard rocks with three awful-ugly guys."

Of course James took imagined offense right away. "What do you mean, 'awful ugly'?" he wanted to know.

"I mean you three are uglier than just normal ugly, that's what I mean," Rubin responded.

"That ain't even a little bit polite," James said. "You owe us an apology."

"An apology?" Rubin sounded surprised at such a thought.

"Yes," James said emphatically. "I want to hear you say you're sorry. Prob'ly for the first time in your life too."

"You sure?" Rubin asked.

"I'm certain sure," James answered.

"Okay," Rubin said. "Listen up 'cause here it comes, and I am not going to say it but once."

"Quit blabberin' and say you're sorry," James came back.

Rubin cleared his throat theatrically. "I'm for sure sorry," he said, "that you three are so awful ugly."

The other three laughed, and the bright sun flashed off their silver badges as they rode out.

Seven miles to the south Joel gave that familiar flick of the wrist, and his whip cracked just over Peter's head. The lead oxen leaned into the harness, and the wagon began to roll once more.

"Ho, Peter! Ho, Paul!" Joel yelled and settled back into the comfortable routine of another day of moving on. With the reins in hand, threaded through his strong, brown fingers, with his whip close to hand, he was the equal of any man and was as happy and contented with life as he could ever be. Nobody laughed at him when he was being a teamster.

He heard Alvin cussing in back. Alvin wouldn't let him pull off the flour sack and change the dressing on his burned face this morning. It would have hurt sure enough, but if he didn't change the dressing most every day, it would grow tight. Then it would be unbelievably painful to take it off because it would rip off a lot of new-grown skin too.

Joel had just shrugged as Alvin had chased him out. He hadn't really wanted to change the dressing in the first place. It was Alvin who would have to take the pain sooner or later. No skin off Joel's nose. He smiled at the expression.

Alvin had a little better color this morning, and Joel guessed he would pull through. Too bad for Alvin. Too bad for the girl, too, if she wasn't dead already.

"Ho, Paul!" he yelled. "Quit layin' back and pull your weight." He cracked his whip over Paul and was satisfied as the wagon lurched forward. Only a couple more days to Waldo.

If the girl made it, her paw was going to

be plenty hot at Alvin. Even if the girl didn't make it, her paw would want to know why. And then there was Alvin, all primed for a little vengeance. Alvin was of a mind to whip that girl plumb to death, and not real fast, either. Now that would surely be something to see. Life should get real interesting pretty soon, what with one thing or another.

"This here is where they camped last night," Greg said. "They ate two rabbits and some beans then buried their coals and slept over them." He hesitated. "Both in the same bedroll," he finally said.

"So how far are we behind them?" Rubin wanted to know.

Greg walked over the campsite, kneeling to feel the ashes. He took his time, and none of the others rushed him. Greg was thorough, steady, and, most always, right.

"Looks like they breakfasted here, then moved on," he said. "I say we're maybe six hours behind. Seven at most."

James looked disgusted. "You mean we lost an hour on them, don't you?" he asked.

Greg nodded slowly. "Looks that way," he agreed. That was the hour it had taken them to discover which way Watt had doubled back. They had ridden in ever-larger circles from the end of his trail until finally Greg had picked up enough sign to say for sure they were headed west.

Wyatt leaned on his saddle horn. "A lot of this don't make sense to me," he said, slow and measured. The rest listened closely. Wyatt didn't talk a lot, but when he did, he was worth listening to.

"He's been heading east for near two weeks straight. We all know why. Straight line too. No tricks or nothin'." He paused to swing down and sit on a rock, probably the same rock one of them had sat on the night before. "Then he runs into this woman in the middle of nowhere—gotta be a accident on account of no way could they find each other a'purpose out there. Besides, she's in a bad way when they get together."

He started rolling one of his infrequent smokes, taking care not to spill any tobacco. "Then, all of a sudden, he throws a false trail, which pretty easy lets us know he suspects we're followin' him, and heads back in the opposite direction." His match flared, and he puffed easily at his smoke, blowing a small cloud into the quiet air.

The others took the opportunity to take a break also, parking here and there around the old campsite. Watt was getting farther away by the minute, but Wyatt knew that as good as any of them, and he didn't seem to be in any hurry. They all trusted Wyatt, who watched them with interest until they were all seated.

"So I figure he's headed back on account of the girl," he went on. "Maybe she's hurt worse than we figured and he has to get her to a doctor."

"That would explain him sleeping with her," James butted in. "It just didn't seem like Watt for him to do that."

"Don't forget it was almighty cold here last night," Greg pointed out. "Maybe they only got one bedroll."

"If that's the case, I guess maybe Watt didn't get such a good night's sleep, neither," Rubin said, and they all smiled as they thought that over.

Wyatt waited patiently until they were finished.

"Might be he just doesn't want her along when he does what he's fixin' to do," he began again. "Whatever the reason, he's going west on account of her, and that means he's going to leave her someplace before he goes ahead with his plan." He gave the others a moment to think on that, then went on. "He knows we're behind him, so he'll probably set a couple more tricks and traps before he gets to where he's going. These will doubtless fall us even farther behind than we are now."

The rest of them could easy see the sense in that.

"I think we should figure where he's goin' and just head straight there instead of following along, doin' whatever he makes us do." Watt leaned back, took a final drag on his smoke, and ground it out. He was almost finished.

"I thought on it a while," he said, "and I believe he's headed for that town we were in last, Waldo. If we ride straight from here, we should be there afternoon tomorrow. Maybe we can surprise him." It was quiet around the camp for a while as they all thought that over. Then they swung back onto their horses. They sat there for another minute and studied the pretty campsite.

"They slept together right here, huh?" Rubin asked.

Greg nodded. "Yup," he said.

A long pause. Rubin looked around. "Sure is a pretty campsite," he said.

"We can still get in three hours of riding before sundown," James pointed out.

"That puts us right back in the middle of nothin', doesn't it?" Rubin said.

" 'Fraid so," James answered.

"See," Rubin said with a theatrical sigh. "I told you he was picking our campsites for us." He kicked his horse into motion, and they headed off to the southwest, ignoring the plain trail to the west Watt had left from the camp.

What they couldn't know was that Watt had headed west for only a mile before he, too, turned direct for Waldo. He knew the men who were following him, knew they would figure him out once they reached the campsite, knew they would head straight for Waldo. He held on to his slim seven-hour lead.

He was cutting it close, but couldn't see any other way to get Rachel back to her father. Besides, he could use some supplies.

A day and a half due east of Waldo fifteen other riders ate up the ground at a lope. Randy McKnote headed up the group, followed by four of his best hands. He rode like a man on a mission, and he was.

The owner of the second biggest ranch in Nogero County hadn't gotten where he was by dodging trouble. All his life he had taken

it head on, and that was what he was fixing
to do now. It wasn't for him to cower in his
home surrounded by hired hands when
there was fighting to be done. He reined in,
took off his hat, and wiped his forehead with
his sleeve. He took time for a sip from his
canteen too. He was tired some, but he
wouldn't let it show to his men.

McKnote was in his late forties now, and
Rosalie's fine cooking had sort of dropped
his chest into a small but annoying paunch
that hung over his belt. He had seen the
same thing happen to others as they aged,
but that didn't mean he had to like it any.

His hair had silvered at the temples and
plain disappeared down the center of his
head, but he didn't feel old. He still felt eighteen inside and sometimes thought eighteen. It was the thinking eighteen that had
caused all this trouble in the first place.

It would please him to apologize and
make it up to the young man, but somehow
he didn't think that was going to happen.
In a way he couldn't blame Mr. Watt at all.
He'd have probably done the same thing
back when he was younger. Heck, he might
even do the same thing today if the positions
were reversed.

And because he understood, he knew. One

of them was going to be dead. Soon. And that meant it had to be Mr. Watt because he wasn't ready to leave Rosalie and the ranch. Not yet, anyway.

"Want to camp here, Mr. McKnote?" Sam asked. McKnote looked at him. Sam had been along for the whole ride. They had started together, fought side by side, aged together too. There was some fatigue behind Sam's eyes, and McKnote felt for him. But there was something he had to do, and the sooner it was over, the sooner they could all get back home.

"Not yet, Sam," he said quietly.

Sam nodded. He knew too.

McKnote carefully placed his hat on his balding head and booted old Trotter into action. The fifteen men strung out as they followed somebody's wagon tracks westward.

The blacksmith fit the mold. He was bulky, especially around the neck and shoulders, built up from years of hammering and pulling on the big leather bellows. Not real tall, his battered leather apron reached clean to his ankles and showed a multitude of scrapes and scars from flying sparks and drops of hot metal.

He had apprenticed with the well-respected Joshua Weems, working diligently under his constant screaming and hollering for seven long years. At times he had wanted to chuck it all, to throw down the apron and stalk out of the shop and out of the world of smithing, but he hadn't. The idea of taking a useless piece of metal, all hard and unyielding, heating it to pliability and then hammering and twisting it into something useful had appealed to him deep where he lived. He had stuck it out and learned, and at the end of his apprenticeship Joshua had shaken his hand and told him he was the best he had ever trained.

He'd have been a big-city smith, too, only there was that trouble with Lily and the drummer, trouble his strong hands had put a harsh and violent end to almost without any thought on his part. He thought on it occasionally, on how surprised he had been at how soft people were and how easily broken as he had looked down on them. And then he left and wound up in the nowhere town of Waldo, a town that barely was a town before he arrived and was now a town that bragged about him as one of its main services.

Of course, there were not many to use his

services out in the middle of nothing like they were, but he lived pretty well on the income from the mine owners, the miners themselves, and the occasional itinerant wanderer.

It was always the wanderers who fascinated him. They would come riding in, mostly alone, settling comfortably on their horses. It seemed like they always had good, sound horses, no matter how scruffy the rest of their outfits. They most always had clean guns too.

He tried to put stories to them sometimes, tried to imagine what in their lives had pushed them out of the regular world and into their lonely existence. Most of the stories he guessed at were romantic because that's what drove him to wander himself. Some of the stories were violent and involved guns and mayhem.

This one, though, was different. He had ridden up from the southwest and was slim like all the rest, only he was dressed real good, with a coat and vest under his long duster. He had a worn Colt in his holster, and the butt of a new Winchester stuck out of the boot. His face was slim, and his blue eyes looked at a man straight and good, as if studying on what was behind the man, pushing him on.

Jebb didn't mind being examined because he was doing some examining himself.

"Howdy," he said.

"Hello." The man looked around the small shop. "Grain for my horse and look to his front shoes."

Jebb nodded. "Sure thing, mister," he said. "New shoes are a dollar a hoof."

The man nodded. "How soon can you be finished?" he wanted to know.

"Got to finish what I'm doing," Jebb said and pulled on the bellows for emphasis. "Then I can take care of him. Be finished in about two hours."

"Fine." The man dismounted and handed the reins to Jebb. He slid the Winchester from the boot. "Anyplace to eat in this town?" he wanted to know.

"Hotel."

"Any good?"

"Only place in town," Jebb answered.

A slight smile cracked the man's face. "I see," he said and turned to go. He stopped. "You hear of or see a man named Watt around here lately?"

"Went through town about five days ago,"

Jebb told him. "Killed a man before he left, though."

The stranger turned back, interested. "He kill a rancher?"

"Naw. Just some miner gave him no choice." Jebb wasn't real put off by the killing. "That miner asked for it good and proper. Man has to know his shortcomings, and the miner didn't figure Watt was as good as he really was. 'Course, nobody else in town had figured on him bein' that good, neither."

The stranger smiled a hard smile at that, swung the Winchester over his shoulder, and walked out toward the hotel.

Watt was kind of tired. He hadn't slept real well the night before and probably wouldn't sleep real well tonight, either. They came up on the only clump of trees for miles around, and it was a little early to stop, but he did, anyway. He rode into the trees, swung his leg over Horse's head, and slid to the ground. He turned and lifted Rachel down. The thought entered his mind to pull her close, wrap his arms around her and hold her warm and close, but he thought better of it. It probably wouldn't suit her at all.

Horse blew, and his breath was steaming in the cold. Watt hoped the men behind them would be plenty cold tonight, sleeping out in the open like they would be. They should at least be as tired and uncomfortable as he was.

Rachel started gathering tinder for the fire, and he remounted and slid his Winchester out.

"Going for meat," he said. "Won't take long."

She nodded and kept on working as he rode out.

He was an unusual man to Rachel. Quiet. Solid. A good man. Not at all like Alvin. Or like Paw, either, as far as that was concerned. He sure wasn't like the men Paw had warned her about. Could be Paw only told her about the bad ones and never mentioned that there were good ones around. She remembered Alvin. He sure fit Paw's description. Could be that there just weren't very many good ones.

Of course there was that moment there, when he lifted her down, that she thought he might just hold on to her and pull her close and hold her to him. But he hadn't. She had never really been hugged by anybody but Paw and wondered what it would have been like to be held by another man, to be hugged front to front like that in the cold, fresh air. She was a little disappointed he hadn't done it.

The fire caught, grew, and she huddled close for a minute, warming her hands. She looked around, wishing Watt—Mr. Watt would get back. She was surprised to realize she missed him, even more surprised to find out she was worried about him. Funny how he had become such a central person in her life when she hadn't even known he existed only two days before.

She cocked her head as she heard the bark of his rifle in the distance. That got her moving again. She got water from a small spring and started the coffee boiling. Watt would like her having it ready for him when he got back. It was the kind of thing a woman did for a man.

Even though she was waiting for him, his sudden appearance surprised her. He had a small antelope thrown across the saddle. It looked like they would have some meat with their beans tonight. Rachel had found his jar of sourdough starter and some flour, and there were biscuits in the pan, already cooking.

"We're going to feast tonight, Mr. Watt,"

she said. She kept her voice calm although she was almighty glad to see him.

"Smells good already, Rachel," he said as he swung down. "I'll slice off a couple of steaks here, and you can get to cooking, if you don't mind."

"It's about time you let me earn my keep," she responded. "I do so hate being a burden."

Watt followed words with action, and it was almost no time before she had the steaks searing over the open fire. Mr. Watt was going to be surprised. He thought of her as a girl, but she had been cooking for Paw for five years now and was proud of her ability. She could cook for a man real fine.

Watt put up Horse and hung the antelope in the tree for the night. He figured to eat off it again at breakfast, then leave it there and the four men behind would maybe stop and eat from it too.

"Supper is ready, Mr. Watt," Rachel said. She was kneeling across the fire, working with the food, and he could smell the rolls and coffee. She looked natural over there. Like she belonged. He knew he was going to miss her.

The second stranger in the same day surprised Jebb at his forge something awful.

He had always had some kind of sixth sense that warned him when someone was coming, but this one just suddenly was there, standing quiet and calm in the door like he had been there all along. In spite of himself, Jebb startled when he first saw him there.

"Sorry," the man said in a quiet voice. "Not trying to sneak up on you."

"It's all right," Jebb said. "Just so busy I didn't hear you coming." The man looked at the other stranger's big horse, eyes taking in the new shoes on the forefeet.

He was tall as the first stranger, but his clothes were not so nice. He looked the part of a cowhand in from the range, only he didn't have the look of deviltry that most of them had. His eyes were shaded by the overhang of his hat, but his face was lean and bronzed deep by the sun. His rolled-up sleeves showed the long sleeves of his undershirt, and his hands hung easily at his sides. His leather vest was worn but serviceable. His gun was clean.

"Place is getting pretty busy," Jebb said. "You're the second stranger here today."

The man didn't appear to show much interest at that. "Put my horse up for the night?" he asked.

"Ten cents. Twenty-five with grain," Jebb answered.

"That's fine. Which one of those is the hotel?"

"Last one on the left." Jebb pointed at the single-story structure.

"Obliged," and the man dropped his reins, shucked his Winchester, and walked through the shop and out the front toward the hotel.

The hotel was about what you'd expect in Waldo. A saloon, really, because that's where the money was made, with five rooms in back. The only people whoever used the rooms were visitors to the mine, drummers and such, or clients for the blacksmith. All were empty at the moment.

The front door, bragging real frosted glass from halfway up clean to the top, closed softly behind the stranger. Six miners were playing poker at a table, and they looked up for a moment, took him in, then went back to their game. A lone man sat in the back corner table, eating, his Winchester lying across the chair to his right, close at hand. He didn't appear to pay the newcomer any mind.

Glen laid his rifle across the bar, and the bartender came right up.

"Howdy," the bartender greeted. He was a short man, on the scrawny side, but when he was behind the bar, he was as big as anyone else because he had built a platform that ran the length of the bar. Fifteen years in the business had taught him well, and he could judge men when they came to his bar, judge whether they were drummer or cowhand, well off or poor, talkative or quiet, hard or soft. This one was probably a cowhand with a dollar or two to spend, but he wasn't the frisky type like they were when they came in in bunches.

"Howdy," the quiet man said. He didn't speak loudly, but Steve could hear him real good, anyway.

"Whiskey?" Steve asked.

"You got fresh coffee?" he wanted to know.

"Sure do. Just made some for him," and Steve indicated the man eating in the dim corner.

"Real coffee?"

"Sure is."

"I'll have some," the stranger said.

Too bad. Steve made his money on the whiskey. 'Course, maybe this fellow was only going to start with coffee. He fetched him a cup from the kitchen, and the man put a nickel on the bar before he sipped at the stuff. A look of satisfaction.

"That's fine," he said.

"You here for the excitement, huh?" Steve asked. Maybe he could find out something about the man if he gave something first.

"What excitement?"

"The Watt trouble," Steve said.

The man looked at him over the coffee. Steve thought he looked familiar somehow, although he couldn't place him just yet.

"Yeah," he explained. "Man named Watt came through here a few days ago. Killed a man, then rode on out. Day later four lawmen come through looking for him. Now we got word he's headed back here with some woman he found out there, and the lawmen are no doubt right behind. Around here, we call that excitement."

"Sounds interesting," the man said, then, "How much for a room and some supper?"

"Room is fifty cents. Beans and bread are twenty-five cents, or a steak is fifty cents."

"You get beans with the steak too?"

"Sure thing. Beans, bread, and fried potatoes."

"I'll have the steak and a room."

"Sure thing. That'll be one dollar and a nickel for the coffee."

The man dug a silver dollar out of his jeans and placed it carefully on the bar next to the nickel.

An honest and hard-earned dollar and a nickel, Steve thought. He took the coins. "I'll need a name for the register," he said.

"Glen," the man said in his soft voice. "Glen Watt."

Steve's expression didn't change as he carefully wrote the name in his register. Glen Watt! This was getting more and more interesting all the time.

"I'll be going for my saddlebags," Glen said.

Steve nodded. "I'll keep an eye on your Winchester till you get back," he said.

Glen pulled the door closed behind him.

One of the miners, Walter, looked up from the table. "That man say his name was Watt?" he asked.

The stranger in the corner looked up, suddenly interested.

"That's right," Steve said. "Glen Watt."

"Whooee!" Walter crowed. "Going to be a hot time in the old town tomorrow, huh? Two Watts going up against four rangers!"

"We're playin' cards here," Roger said in a disgusted voice. He was obviously losing.

The stranger in the corner rose and

walked toward the door. "I'll be right back," he said. "Just leave everything where it is."

Steve nodded. Part of him wanted to follow. Part of him figured he was a lot better off if he just stayed behind his bar.

Chapter Three

"This is great," Watt said, his voice muffled some by a mouthful of antelope steak. Whenever he cooked meat, he just threw it in the skillet and cooked it until it was done clean through, but Rachel had seared the meat over the fire and never even put it in the skillet at all. It was juicy, slightly pink inside, and tasted of the salt she had sprinkled on. Besides, he was hungry.

"Thank you, Mr. Watt." She said it calmly, but was secretly quite pleased at the compliment. She cooked well, and she knew it. She'd *had* to learn to cook well, or Paw had smacked her with his leather belt for wasting food.

"Mr. Watt?" she said, a little unsure.

"Mmppff," he grunted around another mouthful.

"I don't feel right calling you Mr. Watt all the time. Surely you have a Christian name."

"Name's David," he said. "Most folks call me Davey." Actually, most folks called him Watt. Only family ever called him Davey.

"Davey," she said, as if trying it out. "Davey. It sounds so lighthearted for a man who is so serious."

He shrugged. "Some men have lots of reasons to be serious," he said before he took time to think about it.

She looked at him across the fire, wondering about what his problems could be.

Davey forked the last of his beans into his mouth and handed her the plate, fork, and his big knife. "Here," he said. "Your turn."

Rachel plopped her steak from the skillet to the plate, spooned out some of the beans and, using their only fork and knife, began her supper. She was pleased with herself. She had fed her man first, and he was satisfied.

Davey sipped at his coffee and leaned back on one elbow. Rachel was concentrating on her eating, and he watched her, just enjoying the sight of a woman at ease in his camp. A man could get used to having a woman around to watch, specially one who could cook meat so well. The cooking would be nice. The watching was nothing to sneer at, either.

They were so different from men, so smooth-looking and soft and dainty in their actions. A woman's form was something every man delighted in, and Davey was no exception. He had been all too aware of Rachel's womanness since she had first showed up, taken by her shape when she didn't even know he was looking at her; her straight back when she walked and the not-so-straight lines of her front; the smoothness of her neck and that unforgettable glimpse of her slim legs when she mounted Horse. All these things about her were wonderful and brought the years of aloneness right up into a keen wanting.

But to have such a woman really care about a man, have her want to hold a man close, warm him and love him—well, that was something so fine, so wanted, that it was beyond the ken of a plain man like him. That only happened for other men, men who lived another kind of life in another kind of world.

In Davey's world, life was meant to be lived alone. It wasn't his choice anymore. It seemed like the choice had been made when he was born, because he was gifted with *the* hands that were fast, ever so fast, and the early occasion to use them.

The first one had been easy because it was life or death for his father, and the three men hadn't really figured that a fourteen-year-old boy could use the gun that seemed so big on him. He and his dad had shot them all full of holes, and they paid the full price of their evil ways; only father had, too, and then Davey was all alone in the world. A fourteen-year-old boy with a reputation and a memory that tore at him, a memory of the buck of a gun in his fist and the awful result as another man died, his insides smashed to pieces.

His brothers had already spread to the winds, so he, too, had ridden away, and in the next town, Dover, that stupid sixteen-year-old had faced him down in the street and made him draw, and when it was all over, Davey had another haunting memory and a name for himself that he did not want.

It kept on that way, from town to town and job to job. No matter what, whether punching cows or laying track or clerking, somebody would recognize him sooner or later. Then somebody else would want to try him, and Davey would be cornered into using his talent again and another awful memory would be added to the pile. There were nine of them now, the last that stupid miner in Waldo who could not have known who Davey was. It was such a stupid way for a man to die, trying to prove how fast he was with a gun, just to impress some drunken friends. And to pick on a stranger like he had done, to pick on an unknown, was really dumb, and he had paid the price and Davey would have to carry the burden. Until it was his turn.

It was like his life was all planned out for him beforehand on account of his talent. He had never set out to shoot anybody on purpose. Until now.

When he heard that little Markie had been hanged in Nogales County for horse stealing, he had first been heartbroken. Little Markie was his brother Jefferson's only child, and he was twelve years old when he was hanged. The boy was a little slow in the head, but there was no way he had been involved in any horse stealing.

Davey couldn't imagine what the kid was doing so far from home, but his grief had turned into hard anger at the man who could see fit to hang a twelve-year-old boy and call it justice. McKnote was his name, and he was a rancher and had killed a Watt unjustly, and he would not make that mistake again.

"More coffee, Davey?" Rachel broke into his reverie, and he held up his cup for her to fill.

"We should make Waldo about noon, I figure," he said.

Rachel looked at him for a long moment, blue eyes unreadable. "All right," she responded. It wasn't much of an answer and didn't even begin to hint to Davey the sudden flood of emotion his announcement brought on.

So, it would be over. By noon the next day. And he would get back on his big horse, on Horse, and nod and ride away, and she would never see him again. All this togetherness that had seemed so strange and threatening at first now seemed so natural. But it would be over, and he would be gone. She would once again be a girl at her father's beck and call instead of a woman working together with her man.

Rachel analyzed her feelings, startled at thinking of Davey as her man. That was foolish. He was just a man. Three days together didn't make him her man.

Three days ago she hadn't even wanted a man, except to be back with Paw. She hadn't thought she would ever want to be with a man or spend the rest of her life with him. She hadn't even thought that a man like Davey could exist. Now, here she was, feeling awful inside because she was going to lose him. Forever.

She sat down and fumbled with a tattered strip of her dress. "I'd best fix this dress before we get there," she said to him.

"Couldn't hurt," was his answer. "You can wear my duster if you want."

She took his long duster from where it was lying on the saddle and stepped out into the rapidly darkening trees. His duster felt pretty rough against her bare legs when she walked back into camp, dress in her hand. She took the needle and thread from the saddlebag and sat down by the fire.

Her dress was such a mess, almost shredded down the front, she didn't think she could make it whole again. Maybe presentable, though, at least enough so she could keep her dignity when they got into the town. Davey was watching her as she worked, but she didn't mind at all.

Far off in the trees a bird called into the dusk, a lonesome, plaintive cry. Once, twice, three times it called; then silence descended on the small grove, silence broken only by the sound of the wind in the trees and the occasional crack of the fire.

It was already cold, the wind biting through anyplace it could. Rubin looked morosely into the small fire struggling against the cold wind. He thought more heat than he could actually feel from the fire.

"Throw some more wood on the fire," he told James.

"Sure. You go get it first." He was right. There wasn't a tree for miles in any direction.

"I told you he was picking our campsites for us," Rubin complained. "I'll bet he's got trees and water and a big fire to keep him warm."

"And a woman," Wyatt said. That quieted them some, thinking of Watt with the woman.

"Don't make much sense, a woman being out here all alone like that," Greg said to nobody in particular.

"Gotta be an interesting story behind that, all right," Rubin responded.

"She's lucky she came across a man like Watt, actually," Wyatt observed. "Most other men might not have been so honorable, if you know what I mean."

James snorted. "If he's so all-fired honorable, how come we've been chasing him for three weeks?"

"You can't start thinking like that," Rubin responded. "It ain't our job to start figuring on who's good and who's bad. It's for us to bring them in. It's for the judge to figure them out."

"I'm not so sure that's right in this particular case," Wyatt came back. "We all know Walters was the judge's brother."

"Every family has its black sheep," James observed.

"Well, it just didn't sound like murder to me," Wyatt said. "More like self-defense. It ain't like Watt to murder anybody."

"Counting that miner, he has sent at least nine men to their eternal reward," Rubin observed. "Even if Walters wasn't murder, one of them probably was."

"If you're saying that he deserves to hang, anyway, that ain't the way the law is supposed to work," Wyatt came back. They could tell he felt strongly about this. "I got my doubts," he went on, "that Watt is going to get a fair chance in front of the judge."

"I told you," Rubin said, "it's not for you to judge. It's for you to catch him."

"I'm not that simple a man," Wyatt said with quiet dignity. "I have broke bread with Watt. You all have. I know he did not murder that man." He paused for a long time. "And so do you all," he finally clapped end to his argument.

"The warrant says murder," Rubin came back. "That means he's coming back with us. Dead or alive." The wind blew cold into Rubin's clothes, and he shivered and tried to get closer to the diminishing fire. "Dang that Watt," he said. "I'm likely to freeze solid."

"I don't think he would mind," James said.

Glen heard the footsteps coming along behind and kept on walking. If it was trouble, he would know soon enough, and he was ready. He was always ready.

He got his saddlebags from the smithy's and headed back out toward the hotel. The man waiting for him in the dusk was easy to see.

"Glen," he called.

Glen stopped. The voice sounded friendly, but that didn't mean anything.

"Glen, it's me. Jefferson."

Jefferson. His brother. Little Markie's father. Glen's hand streaked down for his gun, and the loud bang of a forty-five woke the sleepy town of Waldo.

The icy wind blew hard around the little grove, but the trees seemed to sap its bite and in where they were camped, there was much noise but little fury from it. Rachel sewed by firelight, and Watt finished the last of the coffee, then got his little shovel and dug the trench for the coals that would heat the bedroll through the long night.

"That's a clever way to prepare a bed, Davey," she said as she sewed. It still startled him to have her call him Davey. It had been so long since anyone called him that.

"You live out here alone long enough, you learn a few things," he said. "Tell the truth, I set more than one bedroll on fire before I learned how to do it right. That's a very fast way to wake up in the middle of the night."

Rachel laughed out loud, and he thought it sounded almost like music to him.

He took several shovels of coals and spread them throughout the small trench, then covered them with just enough dirt so the heat could come through but the bedding would not catch fire. That done, he threw more wood on the fire and spread the bedroll out over the trench to warm some.

"Is it time to go to bed?" Rachel asked. "I still have a little more sewing to do here."

"Not yet, Rachel. I intend to build a lean-to over the bedroll on account of the snow."

"Snow?"

"It's going to snow tonight, I think, and I don't care to wake up all wet."

"Good idea," she said and went back to her sewing while he bustled about, building the lean-to.

Davey worked slow and steady, carefully weaving pine boughs for the roof, trying to make it as tight as possible. Then he gathered extra wood for the fire and stacked it close at hand. He could see Rachel's breath as she worked with numb fingers, so he built up the fire as much as he could and watched her sew for another ten minutes.

"I'll turn in now," he said. A slight pause, then, "We'll be needing that duster over the blanket tonight."

"Almost finished," she said. "I'll spread it over us."

He pulled off his boots and hung them

upside down on two sticks stuck in the ground, then his gunbelt, which he laid close at hand beside the bedroll. The blankets were toasty warm, and he stretched like a cat, luxuriating in the warmth, fully comfortable for the first time all day. Lean and tough as he was, the almost sinful comfort of first crawling into a warm bedroll on a cold night sometimes made the harsh days easier to endure. He rolled onto his left side so there would be room for her behind him when she came to bed.

He closed his eyes and listened to her humming softly across the fire. He heard her get up and then heard the unmistakable sounds of her taking off the duster. Her footsteps came closer, and suddenly she was there, gently laying the duster on top of him. She slid into the bedroll next to him, inevitably touching him here and there with her body as she did so, then rolled on her side like him. He could feel her there, not touching him at all, but only an inch away, nested together like warm spoons in a drawer.

"Mmmmmm," she said almost directly into his ear. "This feels heavenly."

He assumed she was referring to the warmth of the bedroll. He didn't respond.

"Davey?" she said finally. "You awake yet?"

"Yes."

"It's nice and cozy in your lean-to."

Davey didn't think this was a real good time for a conversation, so he merely grunted.

"This is our final night together, isn't it?" she asked, real quiet. The fire sputtered red light and heat into the lean-to.

"Probably," he answered, eyes open wide in the dim light.

"I want to thank you, then," she said. "You saved my life and took care of me when I needed you."

"Anybody would have done the same thing."

"Maybe," she said, "but I'm glad it was you." Her small arm reached around his shoulder, and she pulled herself to him, fitting her entire length to his in a long hug. "Thank you, Davey Watt," she said as she held him to her. Then she released him and slid back away.

For Davey it was a moment he would be able to pull out of his memory at will for the rest of his life, and he knew it. Her softness, her gentle fitting of herself to his form, her small arm holding him against her, were all etched hard and firm into his mind.

He wanted to turn and face her and pull her to him so strong, the feeling almost got away from him, but he thought on it with the only part of his mind that was still thinking at the moment. Thought on it and realized if he did, he would be no better than the man who drove her into the wilderness in the first place. He held himself stiff and tight and didn't make the move his entire being was crying for.

"You're welcome, Rachel," he said.

Jefferson's instincts had saved him, and he had dropped to the dirt the instant he had seen Glen's hand drop to his gun. He had heard the hum of the slug as it passed over him and was surprised to find his own forty-five in his hand and lined up on his brother's form.

"Glen!" he called desperately. "Don't shoot. It's me. Jefferson." His brother stood stock still as Jefferson looked at him down the length of his gun barrel.

The bang of the forty-five had startled Glen almost as much as Jefferson. He had just tried to kill his own brother! The realization slammed home with brutal force and shock. His own brother! With shaky hand he dropped his gun back into his holster.

"Oh, cripes, Jeff," he said, his voice shaky. "I'm sorry. I'm sorry. I don't know what got into me. Are you okay?"

Jeff was getting to his feet. "You never could shoot worth a darn when you hurried like that," he muttered.

"I have never been gladder I missed," Glen said. "I'm sorry as I can be, Jeff. I don't know why I did that."

"Sure you do," Jeff said, still annoyed. "You thought I was going to kill you. Well, I got news for you; unlike some others I could name, I do not shoot my own brother." He took a step toward the hotel where they could see the form of a man framed in yellow light as he looked out curiously from the open door.

"Let's walk side by each back to the hotel," Jefferson went on sarcastically.

"I said I was sorry!" Glen responded.

"And I believe you, too." Jeff came back, "But my heart is beating so fast, and I'm so nervous that anybody stepping along behind me best have made his peace with the Lord and all living things."

Glen fell into step alongside, berating

himself mightily. How could he think that solid, steady Jeff would shoot first and ask questions later, especially when it was his own brother? Besides, after what had happened, Glen figured he deserved to stand there and take the shot instead of making any attempt to fight back.

The bartender stepped aside as they approached the door, an unspoken question in his eyes.

"Gun went off," Jeff explained, then brushed past the man and went back to his table. He dropped into his chair and resumed eating.

Glen sat down opposite. "You don't appear to be real nervous anymore to me," he said.

"I got over it," Jeff said around a mouthful of steak.

Steve, the bartender, brought over Glen's food and plunked it on the table in front of him. He refilled their cups, then went back to his bar and his elevated walkway. In a way he wished he could stay and listen; in another way he figured he might be better off not hearing.

Glen's steak struggled back against the knife. Tough. Old range cow, most likely, with all the toughness left in. After what he had just tried to do, he deserved tough meat.

"Davey should be here tomorrow, most likely," Jefferson said.

"How's everybody know that?" Glen asked. He was starting to get his emotions under control once more.

"Indian came through here early this morning."

"What's the deal with the lawmen?"

"They got a murder warrant for him," Jeff explained.

"Murder?" Glen was surprised. "Davey wouldn't murder anybody."

"You know that," Jeff said, "and I know that. They were not so sure, I guess." They ate in silence for a while.

"Indian said Davey had a woman with him," Jeff threw out.

Glen's eyebrows reached for the top of his head. "Davey has a woman?" he asked. "He's barely a man himself! What is this world coming to?"

"He's twenty-five years old," Jefferson pointed out. "I reckon that's man enough." He took his last bite of steak and chewed pensively while he studied his younger brother.

Glen hadn't changed much since he was

a kid. He had a few wrinkles that came natural as a man aged into his thirties, but his eyes were still the same, and obviously his attitude was still a little flighty. He always had a habit of acting before thinking, and, in a way, Jefferson was a little surprised that Glen hadn't wound up in jail or worse.

He had always loved Markie like he was his own, though, and on his infrequent stops at the ranch Markie's eyes would light up and pure joy would flow through his veins. Probably because they were both still kids, Markie on the outside and Glen on the inside. They would ride out into the hills together and camp and play games, and Markie would have cheerfully died for his Uncle Glen.

Markie didn't have many friends, because of his slow ways, but Uncle Glen could be counted on to brighten his days and put joy and maybe even some meaning into his life. That was why Jefferson had no trepidations about letting Glen take Markie on such an extended trip. Even if he would have had some worries, the hanging of his son would not have been one of them.

When Emmett had ridden out from town and told him, Jefferson had refused to believe it. Markie dead? Not a chance. But he had produced the letter from the sheriff at Fort Atkinson, and the letter spelled it out so plain and straight that there could be no mistake, and Jefferson had to accept that he was alone once more, that the childlike laugh and upturned nose and shock of uncombed yellow hair were gone forever. Buried under the earth in Fort Atkinson, Nogales County. Buried among people who didn't know him and who wouldn't care about him. Hanged out in the country without a friend to comfort him. Hanged by mistake, was the wording in the letter. And no word had ever come from Glen. No word at all.

"What happened?" Jefferson asked softly.

Glen's face changed visibly. He aged as the look of pain and sorrow added wrinkles and years and stole the joy from him.

"I haven't been able to talk about it," he said so softly Jefferson could barely hear him. "Not to anyone. Least of all, you."

"I have to know, Glen," Jefferson responded. "I have a right to know. You have to tell me."

"We were camped five miles north of Fort Atkinson with the new herd we bought. Ten of the finest horses you could ever find. Bill of sale all proper and legal. But the man who sold them to us didn't own them. He signed the right name on the bill of sale. McKnote. I never suspected anything." He took a deep breath and sipped at his coffee. Jeff saw his hands tremble.

"It had been a great adventure for Markie. You should have seen him, Jeff, all happy and proud of all he had learned about traveling and setting up camp and reading weather." He looked Jefferson in the eye for a minute, then dropped his gaze once more. "There wasn't anything slow about him when it came to being out in the wilderness. It was the happiest I have ever seen him." He stopped for a drink of coffee, sighed a big breath, and let his mind take him to where he didn't ever want to go again.

"I was having a good time too," he went on. "But you know how I am, Jeff. I get older, but sometimes I still think young and stupid. This was one of those times." He closed his eyes and saw the whole thing clear as crystal on the inside of his eyelids.

"I knew Fort Atkinson was only a short ride away, and I knew there was a saloon and women there. We set up camp early in the afternoon just so I could do what I did. We had already been out in the wild for two weeks, and I figured nothing could possibly happen to him where we was camped, so I told him I'd be back real late, and into town I went."

"You left him there?" No accusation in the tone, just a question.

"He didn't want to go," Glen explained. "I asked him earlier if he wanted to go into town and spend the night at the hotel, but his face fell and he said he didn't know any of the people there and didn't care to go among them."

"I see," and Jefferson did see. Markie never liked being around strangers because somehow they would always know. They would always know, and even if they didn't say anything, Markie knew they thought of him as something different, something a little less than human. He was real sensitive, and he always knew.

"I think he actually wanted me to go," Glen went on. "Wanted to spend some time alone in the wild. A great big adventure for him to be all alone out there."

Jefferson nodded. Yup. Markie would like that, all right.

"I rode back, and it was just after sunup when I got to the camp. There were lots of tracks, and they had spent the night and eaten most of our food and coffee. Markie was gone, and so were they. I trailed them a mile north, where I rode over a small hill and—" His face trembled with the strain, and even with his eyes wide open, he could see the awful picture clear as anything. Sweat beaded on his forehead, and his hands trembled.

"They were all loafing around the tree," he went on, and Jefferson had never seen a sorrier man, a man so tortured and ashamed.

"They were all just resting there." His voice sounded like it came from someone else, someone Jefferson did not know. "They were laughing and talking and acting just like things were perfectly normal." He passed his hand in front of his eyes, but the sight wouldn't go away. "Only, Markie was hanging from that tree," he said. "Hanging there right in the middle of all those men. Hanging there while they laughed and joked and made light of him. Poor Markie who had never hurt any living thing. He had spent the night among strangers who doubtless made fun of him and terrified him and in the red of sunrise hung him until he was dead. And I was in town having a good time."

The agony in his quiet voice stabbed at

Jefferson, and he discovered he was holding his breath. He found it all too easy to imagine his boy's last humiliating, terrifying night. All too easy to imagine Markie's fear of the many strangers. All too easy to imagine the strangers making fun of the boy. Teasing him. Laughing at him. Scaring him with stories of hanging. The pain of grief glowed red and hot and was transformed into anger and hate so bitter and consuming, he could taste it on the back of his tongue.

"I went crazy, sort of," Glen said, and he couldn't look Jefferson in the face. "I don't really remember riding into them, but all of a sudden my gun was empty and one of them shot me off my horse with a rifle. When I woke up, I was in Fort Atkinson, and they told me Markie had been buried good and proper. They told me it had been a mistake and they were sorry." He looked up at Jefferson, and there was no life in his eyes. Not a hint of humanity remained in his gaze.

"I healed up some, and then I went hunting." His voice was flat, with no emotion. "I found the man who sold us somebody else's horses. Found him in a small camp a day's ride from here."

Jeff was stunned. His brother had never looked so hard, so grown up. He was almost scary. He didn't have to ask about the fate of the evil man who profited from his son's death.

"I remember the face of every one of them, Jeff," Glen said. "I will never forget them because I can see them every time I close my eyes. I can see them, and I can always see poor Markie hanging there without a friend. The sight of him will never leave me. I swear to you that each and every one of them is a dead man who is walking yet. I swear." He looked down at his plate. "I swear," he said softly.

Chapter Four

It began with a few soft flakes, gently drifting down through the air like tiny, frosted autumn leaves. They were unseen by the four sleeping lawmen, and some drifted onto the small bed of coals, hissing softly. The temperature dropped steadily as the night aged, and by midnight each breath spilled steam into the hard, cold air. The flakes swelled in size and number, and what had been a gentle, pretty snowfall turned heavy and mean.

Greg woke suddenly, face wet and cold. He could feel the big flakes drop on his face and melt. The fire was not only out, it was covered with a blanket of white.

"Boys," he called. "I think we're in trouble here."

He could hear their muffled exclamations as they woke to the frigid dark and the stark realization that life had once again put them in the face of real danger. They got up, brushed four inches of wet snow from their saddles, and broke camp.

"I told you he was picking our campsites for us," Rubin said. "Now he had maybe gone and killed us that way."

"There you go complaining again," James said. "You don't hear me complaining, do you? Or Wyatt or Greg, neither."

"So what?" Rubin said as he tightened his cinch. He pulled the strap tight and waited for Billy to exhale so he could snug it down. Good horse, only he always held his breath when the cinch was tightened, so the saddle wound up loose. "So I complain," he went on. "Somebody has to do it."

"I wish I was in Waldo so I wouldn't have to listen to all this drivel," Greg said.

"Drivel!" from James. "What do you mean, drivel?"

"I mean listening to the two of you bicker puts me in mind of a old married couple," Greg explained. He put his head through the hole in the center of his blanket and topped it with his slicker and dustcoat. "Nothing to say to each other and too many words to say it with. That is what I call drivel." He tied his hat on with his long woolen scarf to protect his ears from the cold and swung aboard.

"I wish I was in Waldo too," Wyatt said as he mounted. "Lead out of here, Greg. Let's get going before these two drivel us to death."

Greg booted his horse into motion, and they single-filed into the blinding white. The wind was picking up, and that spelled real trouble ahead as it would blow the snow into drifts that would only become deeper as the storm progressed. They were twelve hours from Waldo on a good day. If the snow kept on and the wind picked up anymore, they might as well be two weeks away because they would never make it.

"Drivel!" Rubin mumbled as they rode into the snow. In minutes their tracks were blown full and any trace of their camp was gone forever.

Davey had figured he was in for another night of fitful sleep at best, but had failed to take into account how tired he was. In spite of the warm woman form at his back, or maybe because of it, he dropped into a deep, restful sleep, something he almost never did while out in a camp.

The red firelight flickered shadows on the two motionless forms, neither of which was aware of the first few snowflakes drifting down through the trees and resting on their blanketed forms. As the hours drew out, the fire burned down unseen, and the flakes hissed into the glowing coals more frequently. Their breath steamed into the night, and outside the grove the wind blew harder and the snow fell heavier. In the cold, they moved closer together, and the girl was eventually pressing into Davey's back like a spoon as they shared warmth in the night.

Davey's dreams were exotic and more until he snapped awake, staring into the few glowing coals that remained. Rachel was pressed warm and soft against him, breathing slow and steady against the back of his neck. It was time to build up the fire before it went out, but he lay there for an extra few minutes, allowing his mind to play with the notion of a Rachel who would care for him enough to hold him close when she was awake.

It was passing strange in his mind. Here

he was, closer to a woman than he had ever been, and he had never felt more alone. It was like she was tormenting him with a picture of life that he could never have, and he didn't know whether to pull away at once or make it last, knowing that it was the only set of memories he would have in his life to take out and think on during the long nights to come.

He lay there as long as he could without letting the fire go out altogether, then reluctantly rolled out to restart the fire. He could still feel her warm and soft and pressing into his back as he gently blew the fire back into life, adding bigger and bigger wood until he felt the heat soak into him. The flickering light highlighted her sleeping face, and he looked at her long, fascinated by her smooth skin and the soft pleasantness of her.

She looked so childlike lying there. Childlike and trusting. In him, to take care of her, to protect her and see that she made it safe back to her father. Her paw. And then she would be gone, and he would be alone once more.

An ache worried at his insides when he tried to imagine looking over there and Rachel not being there. Only him, alone in camp once more. Like so many, many nights before. Alone, with nobody to care about him. Nobody to worry when he was away. Nobody to be pleased when he came back. Nobody to hold him close and warm in the cold nights to come.

He felt the want surge through him. The want to go to her and take her in his arms and hold her close to him. The want to feel her put her soft arms around him and hold him close right back. The want to be wanted. By her. By Rachel. Most of all, the want to know she would be there always, be there when things were good or bad, be there through the years to come, be there to trust and be trusted by.

He was suddenly amazed as he realized that he was in love. For the first time in his life. With her. With Rachel. He rocked back on his heels, absorbing that new thought. He pondered on it for several minutes before he tore his mind away and noticed the weather.

The hours dragged by, and the snowfall grew even heavier. Rubin was surprised he couldn't hear it go thud as the big flakes blew against him and Billy. He was following Greg, had been following him for hours, amazed that Greg seemed to know what direction to take because there were no landmarks, no signs to guide them.

The cold had seeped into him slowly, like a sneaky enemy, finding every opening in his bulky clothing. Fingers and toes went numb; then the arms and legs felt cold and the shivering had started. After a while the shivering would stop, and Rubin knew that would be the beginning of the end, a sign his body had given up the fight and surrendered to the cold. His temperature would slowly drift down until unconsciousness set in; he would drop from his horse, and the snow would cover him and he would be gone.

Greg's horse stumbled again; it was becoming more common as exhaustion took the animal. Nothing made of flesh could possibly buck through those drifts for too long without yielding, and Greg's horse was giving out.

What a stupid way to die! A senseless chase after an innocent man. Innocent and pretty darned smart, because he had set them up to die in the middle of nowhere. He had managed to kill all four of them, and he would be blameless. Rubin tried to imagine Watt tucked away safe and secure in a camp somewhere with a woman to keep him company, but he was getting tired and the exercise seemed pointless. Greg's horse stumbled again, and he stopped. Rubin bucked through a drift and came alongside.

Greg's face was almost completely wrapped in his scarf, with only his eyes showing. Icicles hung from the wool where his breath had condensed on the now stiff cloth. Snow was piled on his shoulders and stuck to his cloth coat in front where it had been blowing against him for so long. James and Wyatt formed a circle, and they waited for a momentary lull in the wind so they could be heard.

"Boys," Greg said, "If we can just hold out for seven more months, the sun will be shining, and the grass will be green."

"I keep thinking about Watt in camp with that woman," Rubin said.

"It appears he would be a little smarter than we gave him credit for," Wyatt observed.

"Smarter than us, anyway," James said.

"My horse is giving out," Greg said to nobody in particular.

"How far to Waldo, you figure?" James wanted to know.

"A whole lot too far," Greg responded.

"In that case, how long until summer?" James's voice was muffled by his scarf.

"All the time you got, I'm thinking," Greg answered.

Silence fell around the group as they digested that.

"You want I should lead for a while, maybe give your horse a rest?" Rubin offered.

Greg shrugged. "Why not? Keep the wind in your face, and we should be going in more or less the right direction."

"Well," Wyatt said, "let's move along. I'm beginning to feel a chill from just sitting here."

Rubin looked at his three friends. They had been through so much together. Shame to end like this. He knew it was the last time he would see them or have a chance to speak to them.

"I didn't complain all the time," he said. He turned Billy into the wind and booted him into motion. So many opportunities to die hard and fast. So many risks. He supposed it had to catch up with him sooner or later. Still, this seemed just a little too soon to suit him.

Greg had been right. In seven months it would be warm and the grass would be green and insects would be humming by in the warm breeze. There would be four new sets of bones out here by then. At least they'd finally be warm.

The snow was hitting him in the face, and Billy was plowing through drifts, breaking trail for the three behind, and Rubin knew that was the way he would die. He kept his eyes closed against the driving snow. It was easy enough to steer by the feel of the wind on his front. He hadn't thought it was possible to get any colder, but he did. He allowed his mind to take him back to some of the more pleasant times of his life, and the scenes played like stage shows in his head until finally Billy stopped and wouldn't start again.

Rubin opened his eyes. There was a man on horseback across in front of him. A tall man on a tall horse. A brief lull in the wind.

"Looking for me?" Watt asked.

Alvin lay in the bed and waited for the doctor to come to him. It had been such a long time since he had been in a real bed.

The bartender hadn't seemed real anxious to rent him a room, but in the end had relented, and now he was warm and lying in a soft bed and a doctor would come and he would live. He had no illusions about what she had done to him. His face would be a disfigured mess for the rest of his life. Since he figured on living a long time, he would have to make his vengeance as leisurely as possible because, once over, it would be gone forever and would have to last the rest of his miserable days.

Joel came in without knocking.

"Doctor is on the way," he said. "When I explained about you not letting me change the bandage, he said I should bring you a bottle of whiskey and make you drink it on account of he was going to have to pull that bandage off one way or another."

Alvin groaned in anticipation, and Joel hid his grin. Yessir, this little town of Waldo was sure going to be interesting. He handed a bottle to Alvin, who started drinking frantically. It was plain he wanted to be as oblivious as possible before the doctor got there.

Joel sat there and watched the burned man drink, somewhat enviously. Nobody had ever told him to get drunk on purpose, but when he thought about what was in store for Alvin, he didn't envy him at all. The old doctor was down the hall in the bar, drinking when Joel had found him. He had told Joel to get Alvin drunk and he'd be along in a while.

Doc Wilson downed another shot and watched morosely as Steve made another check on his tab. Pretty soon all his credit earned from medical work would be drunk up, and he would have to limit his drinking to that which he could pay for. He felt no guilt that Steve's woman had died, anyway. Wasn't his fault. The belly pain had come on her and grown worse and worse over a few days; then she had gotten the fever and finally died.

Doc had known she was going to die from the very first, but he kept calling on her and kept billing Steve for it and built up his credit as much as a man could do and still retain some shred of ethics.

Now there was this burned man in room four. With a little luck, Doc could pull him through and maybe get enough cash to keep the liquor covering the memories for a few more days.

"Better give me one more, Steve," he said, then watched as Steve carefully poured the shot glass full. "I need a little fortification," he explained, proud that he could say fortification without slurring. "Burn patients are the worst. All runny and screaming."

Steve carefully marked off another check on the tab. Pretty soon he would be able to throw the drunken old butcher out.

Doc slugged down the shot, part of his mind wondering at the fact that they no longer burned his throat when he did. He took his bag and went rather unsteadily down the hall to room four, where he knocked tentatively on the door.

"C'mon in," from inside.

The smell in the room brought back memories of other unwashed burned patients, and Doc knew it would smell worse before he left, smell worse and be a heck of a lot louder.

The man on the bed looked at him from above a dirty wrapping that used to be an old flour sack. His eyes were terrified, and Doc figured the patient had every right to be scared.

"I ain't ready yet," the man in the bed said, and he held up the almost empty whiskey bottle.

"You're as ready as whiskey will ever make you," Doc said and moved toward the bed. The weird little man with the deformed legs came closer on the other side so he could watch.

The sack had been put on maybe two or

three days ago, and fluid had oozed through it and crusted tight. Doc had seen a lot in his days of medicine, but even his stomach felt a little queasy at what he was about to do. He took hold of the filthy cloth with both hands.

For a moment the man's pleading eyes caught his, and Doc could easily see the abject terror. The patient whined frantically in anticipation.

"Here we go," Doc said.

The snow had been falling in Waldo for about three hours when the line of men rode out of the storm. Fifteen in all, they single-filed from the howling wind and rode to the smithy's barn. Stiff, exhausted, and almost frozen, they swung from their mounts and led them into the shelter of the barn.

McKnote stamped his numb feet on the floor. He was plain worn out and frozen clear through, but grateful. If it hadn't been for his determination to ride straight through, they would all be trapped out in that storm somewhere, all fifteen of them. The wind howled around the barn, but after the hours of exposure it felt warm and protected inside.

His men were also trying to stamp life back into cold limbs, and he could hear them begin to mumble to each other as they gradually came back to life. The place was filled with the smell of horses and the leathery sounds of saddles being removed. The smithy, a man named Jebb as he recalled, came out of the small room where he lived.

"Howdy," he said, and McKnote howdied right back.

"You'll be wanting to board your horses for the night," Jebb said. He was impressed. Business was pretty darn good for such a rotten night. "Price is ten cents a mount, twenty-five cents with grain. Men can sleep here free if they want."

McKnote nodded; price was unimportant. Right now his body was crying for rest. "Grain for the horses," he ordered, then, "How's the hotel?"

"Only got five rooms to start with," Jebb explained, "And four of them are already full."

That didn't set too well with McKnote. Much as he would have loved to go there, it wouldn't be right for him to sleep warm and comfortable while his men were sleeping in the barn.

"We'll bed down here," he said.

"Suit yourself," Jebb said, and he turned to tend to the horses.

A brief lull in the wind left room for the sound of a man's scream, only it was an awful shriek, more like a tormented animal than a man.

The barn was suddenly silent, and McKnote shivered. "What was that?" he asked.

Jebb shrugged. "Doc is working on a burned man at the hotel," he said, and suddenly sleeping in the barn didn't seem like such a bad thing.

The man started screaming again, and then the wind picked up once more and buried the sound of his agony with its cold howl.

"First time all day that wind has sounded good to me," McKnote said.

"Been sounding good to me for half an hour already," Jebb said.

McKnote shivered again. He certainly hoped that doctor wouldn't have to work on him.

Rachel placed another log on the fire and looked around, fretful. It was really snowing hard, big wet flakes that cut visibility down to almost nothing. While protected in the grove of trees, she could easily hear the wind howling outside. Darn that Davey for leaving her alone in weather like this! What if something happened to him?

Her mind went through various scenes of disaster. Davey lying pinned under Horse, slowly freezing to death. Davey fallen and walking, hopelessly lost. She became angry at herself. Davey was a good man, the best she had ever known, and he had taken care of himself in the wild for his whole life. He would be okay.

But it was as if her mind enjoyed tormenting her with horrible thoughts. And the most horrible of all was that she might never see him again. He might fall and be covered, and he would be gone from the sight of men and from her forever. She would never again feel the strength of his presence. Never see the tanned, lean face that she already missed. Never hold him close and warm against her as she had only two hours ago.

She hadn't been asleep when he got up. Far from it. She had awakened earlier to find herself holding him close, warming herself with his lean toughness. Even after he had crawled from their bed to tend the fire, she had felt the memory of him against her. But she had feigned sleep; why she still didn't know. Even when she had felt him looking at her, she hadn't opened her eyes. Could be she had been afraid, afraid of what he might have said or done. More likely she had been afraid of herself and her intentions toward this lone man of mystery.

She had almost held her breath; so many emotions were flooding through her in waves as he softly approached where she lay. He had reached toward her, reached toward her with that tough hand, and she felt fear and anticipation all confused together. He had touched her hair, gently, and she had finally opened her eyes and looked up at him. He had been framed by the red firelight, and his features were invisible. Rachel hadn't known what to do, so she had lain there motionless, looking up at him.

"Blizzard out there," he said. "Some men are in trouble, and I have to go. There's plenty of wood for the fire, and my rifle is right there. I'll be back for breakfast."

Now he was gone. Into the blizzard. And she found herself wishing that she had pulled him down to her and rested his head on her and hugged him and said good-bye, but she had not, and now the moment was passed and he would never know.

And then, there he was again, riding out of the dark with four other snow-covered riders following along behind. The unbearable silence of being by herself was filled with the stomping of tired horses and the audible groans of half-frozen men as they swung down. Rachel stacked log after log on the fire, hearing them sizzle as the snow melted off, and in moments the fire was raging and crackling, and the men crowded around and began to warm the life back into themselves.

Rubin opened his coats and let the red heat soak into his front. He wasn't going to die, after all. Once again death had been cheated, this time by the man he had been sent out to hunt. His three friends were standing, clothes open like him, trying to bring blessed heat back into their chilled selves. They were still too cold to talk, and steam rose from their wet clothes.

Rachel forced her way in between and set a coffeepot on the grate over a small corner of the fire. Davey was bringing their bedrolls and saddlebags into the circle of light as he took care of their horses, and he dropped their bag of food down by the girl. Rubin studied her for a moment as she surveyed their vittles for a minute, then put together a big pot of beans laced with a generous helping of molasses and started slicing some bacon and dropping it into a skillet.

She was wrapped up pretty good, what with the cold and all, but she was young and darned pretty to his eye. She was obviously experienced at feeding men around a campfire. There was a small lean-to with one bedroll in it across the fire from him, and Rubin tried to imagine what it would be like to sleep right next to her like that. She paid attention to her cooking, but he noticed her glance would go over to Watt every chance she got.

Greg stamped his feet, closed his coat, and went to help Watt. He was amazed at how fast their situation had changed. One minute they were doomed and almost dead, the next they were in a good camp with a girl cooking for them and no doubt about their survival. The man responsible for their lives was working at unsaddling their horses while they loafed and warmed themselves at his fire. That didn't set quite right with Greg, and he moved to help set up camp. Somewhat reluctantly, the others followed.

"I told you I would take you someplace safe," Greg said as he dumped another armload of wood by the fire.

"You didn't never," James came back as he was fitting together a lean-to frame. "As I recall it, you seemed to think we were about to become very handsome statues in the middle of nowhere."

"Did not," Greg said and moved to help him. "I never had a doubt that we would survive. I tried to convince you fellers of that, but you were all a little short on backbone and refused to believe me."

"Who's a little short on backbone?" Rubin asked in a dangerous tone of voice as he dropped his saddle.

"I'm sorry if I have offended you," Greg went on, "but I must call them like I see them."

Rubin threw his hands up in the air. "I feel as the Philistines must when confronted by Samson," he declared.

"What do you mean?" Greg wanted to know.

"I have been attacked by the jawbone of an ass," Rubin responded.

They all laughed, even Rachel. She banged on the pot with her spoon.

"Come and get it," she said. They did.

Rubin forked down the last of his plate.

"Ma'am," he said. "those were truly some of the best camp beans I have ever eaten."

"Thank you, sir."

"I thank you, too, miss," Wyatt spoke for the first time. "And I thank you, too, Watt."

Davey looked across the fire at them as they all echoed Wyatt's sentiments. "You boys would have done the same for me," he said, and a strained silence laid out in the camp as they thought about that and what they were there for.

Rachel felt the sudden tension and wondered about it, but was smart enough not to butt in with something inane. Rubin shifted uncomfortably, and his coat fell open. For the first time she noticed the badge.

"It's still snowing, and it looks like we may be here for a day or so," Watt observed. "I suppose we should finish the lean-tos and catch up on some sleep."

"Since there's no hurry anymore, I sure would favor another cup of coffee first," Greg said.

"Just made another pot," Rachel said and poured his cup to the top.

"Thank you, ma'am," he said.

"Rachel," she said. "You may call me Rachel."

"Always favored the name of Rachel, ma'am," Greg said.

Rachel smiled brightly at him. For some reason, Davey didn't like that much. Rachel filled the other men's cups, and suddenly they weren't in such a hurry to finish work.

And so the long night passed. Five lean-tos faced into the heat of the fire, and six tired people slept the deep sleep of the weary. Outside the grove, the snow fell and the wind howled, and still the temperature dropped. In Waldo, the Watt brothers' sleep soaked into their pillows in rooms two and three, and Alvin slept in the twilight of semi-consciousness, drifting in and out, remembering the interminable agony and feeling the fresh hurt on his face. In the barn fifteen men slept warm and safe, surrounded by the scent of horses and fresh hay.

Fate was carefully setting the scene. In a short span of time, the results would play out.

Rachel woke, slightly cold, and pulled herself up tight against Davey's back once more. Comfortable now, she drifted deeper into sleep, not hearing the howling of the wind or the snoring from the men across the fire. Davey's eyes opened as she pulled against him, and he smiled slightly at the feel of her small arm reaching around him. His eyelids drooped slowly, closed and he, too, slept.

Chapter Five

There was no sun as such in the morning. It grew light, sure enough, but the light was diffused and came from an indefinable source somewhere above the thick clouds.

Rachel presided over thick slices of antelope dangling over the fire from green sticks. Coffee bubbled in the pot, and the smell of fresh coffee and cooking steaks drifted over the still forms of the four strangers. Gradually the four men stirred as hungry bellies growled consciousness back into them.

Davey had already taken his rifle and gone into the woods. One small antelope would not be enough now. His not-too-distant shot jerked all four to their feet, nerves taut. As they came fully awake and remembered the events of the previous day, they relaxed into easy camaraderie once more.

"Ma'am," Rubin said, "you are a sight more pleasant to wake up to than these other three ugly faces, and that's for sure." Rachel smiled up at him, and he realized she was indeed a beautiful young woman.

"Thank you, sir," she said. "You have just earned the first cup of coffee," and she followed words with action and poured some of the steaming hot brew into a metal cup which he took gingerly.

"What do you mean ugly faces?" James asked in feigned anger. "You never said anything all those other mornings when it was one of us handing you the coffee."

"Somehow I don't remember any of you handing me coffee," Rubin came back. "Matter of fact, the last time I can remember any of you waiting on me at all was back when you thought I stood to inherit some money from my Uncle Jack. And as for the ugly faces—why, I'll let the lady decide for herself. Ma'am—Rachel," he said, "aren't these three of the ugliest faces you ever have seen?"

Rachel smiled. She was enjoying the new

company. "I have seen far worse, Mr. . . .
Mr. . . . "

"You can call me Rubin, ma'am," he said.
"And we should be ashamed for not intro-
ducing ourselves sooner. That one down
there who looks like a mule is called Greg,
the one over there who looks like a goat is
Wyatt, and the other one who looks like a
squirrel with a mouthful of nuts is called
James. You will find he is the noisiest one.
You will also find he has the least of value
to say too."

Rachel laughed, delighted. "Tell me,
Rubin," she said, "you find it difficult to
keep friends, do you not?" She was busy
serving coffee to the others, all of whom appeared disgusted with Rubin's introduction.

"Not difficult, ma'am," James said.
"Downright impossible. Only reason we're
with him is account of our chief seen fit to
punish us, and this was the worst he could
think of."

"Humph," Rubin snorted. "Bunch of in-
grates. Here I lead them to safety, and right
away they insult me."

"Seems like Davey might have had something to do with that," Rachel pointed out
as she started putting the steaks on metal

plates and sprinkling salt on them. The men dug in hungrily.

"Davey?" Rubin asked.

"I mean Mr. Watt," Rachel came back very fast. She was embarrassed. The four men took it in, but chose not to make anything of it.

"That's not the way I see it, Rachel," Rubin said around a mouthful of steak. "Hadn't a been for me, why, poor old Watt woulda been lost out there too."

Wyatt snorted. "You have always been a fearful liar," he said. "Meat tastes really fine, ma'am," he added.

The others agreed in muffled tones as they shoveled it in.

The four men stiffened as one and looked off to the north. Rachel looked, too, although she had heard nothing. In a minute she saw Davey moving through the trees, leading Horse. When he got closer, she could easily see the mule deer slung across the saddle. For some reason she was proud of him, proud that her man could easily take care of them all if he had a mind to.

Rubin stuffed the last of his steak into his mouth and went to help Watt with the meat. Rachel hung another steak over the fire for Davey and took him a cup of coffee.

Davey took the cup gratefully, nesting the hot metal in numb fingers. He had been thinking on a cup of coffee all the while he had been waiting for that deer to show itself from behind that big old pine tree. The heat felt good on his hands, and the hot stuff flooded warmth through his insides as he took some of it in.

Rachel was pretty well bundled up but for her face, but just seeing her pretty features, red nose and all, made Watt feel funny in his stomach. He had only been gone maybe an hour, but he had missed her. He knew the sooner he got rid of this girl/woman, the better off he would be, only he couldn't bear to think of her being gone from him. Annoyed, he walked back to camp beside her, all too aware of her next to him.

The men all howdied at him, and he nodded back. Rubin went to work on hanging the deer and butchering, and Rachel sat Davey down by the fire and fussed about getting his breakfast ready. The cooking meat smelled wonderful, and he was suddenly ravenous. Cold weather sometimes did that to a man.

"Kind of a sudden change in the weather, huh?" James asked.

Watt nodded. "Yup," he said, "that's

prob'ly why the storm was so bad. Seems like big changes in temperature always mean bad storms."

"I had noticed that myself," Wyatt said.

Rachel handed Davey his plate. The steak hung over both sides, it was so big. Davey had no doubt he would be able to finish it.

In Waldo the weather brought mixed emotions to almost everyone in town. McKnote was disappointed that the storm would delay the coming action because it meant he would be getting home to Rosalie later than he had figured. On the other hand, it meant nobody would be killed or hurt, at least for a little while longer.

For Jefferson and Glen it was a rare opportunity for them to sleep late, and they did. It was near eight o'clock when they emerged from their rooms and went into the bar for breakfast. Glen finished his eggs, bacon, home-fried potatoes and toasted bread. Satisfied, he leaned back and watched Jeff sopping up the last of his own egg yolk with a piece of toast.

"Poor Davey ain't eating like this, I bet," Glen said.

Jeff grunted, his mouth full.

" 'Course, he is eating with some woman,"

Glen went on. "I don't know whether to feel sorry for him or for me."

In the stable, McKnote's men were ready to go eat. They pushed open the door against the snow and single-filed up the street toward the hotel. McKnote didn't hold out a lot of hope as to the quality of the food. Rosalie had for sure spoiled him.

He took a second to look around the barn now that it was empty. Here and there the bedrolls were lying about where men had passed the night, and the horses moved softly in the straw of their stalls. Jebb came out of his room and looked around.

"Morning," McKnote said.

"Mornin'."

"Just fixin' to go for breakfast," McKnote said. "You care to join us?" The idea sounded pretty good to Jebb.

"Don't mind if I do," he said, and he and McKnote shrugged into coats and walked out, carefully closing the door behind. Up ahead they could easily see the first of their men going into the hotel.

Glen heard the men start coming in, and Jeff watched as they began coming through the door one after another.

"Looks like we got lots of company stuck in town," Jeff observed, and that was the first time Glen turned to look. The color bled from his face, and he turned toward his brother, eyes dead.

"It's them," Glen said. "Them what hung Markie," and he spun back to face the men crowding through the door.

"Damn you!" he yelled. "I'll see you all in hell!" and went for his gun. Others were still coming through the door into the warmth when the first shot blasted out in the quiet bar.

The deer was butchered, more wood had been gathered, the dishes were cleaned, and the third pot of coffee was getting down to grounds. Rachel got water from the stream, marveling at the way the running water steamed into the cold air, and in a few minutes, pot number four was bubbling flavor into the water. It was then she noticed the snow had stopped.

"A man could get used to living like this," Rubin said with a sigh as he watched Wyatt place another log on the fire. "Got somebody else to do the hunting, somebody to fetch the wood, and a pretty woman to do the cooking."

Rachel smiled at him. She was beginning to like Rubin.

"Never did seem like life presented too many problems to you, anyway," James observed.

"Just do my job, and each day takes care of itself," Rubin said.

"Seems like that may present a problem all by itself," Wyatt said flatly, and silence settled on the camp as the five men thought that over.

Rachel felt the strain of the silence and didn't understand it. She didn't like it much, either.

"You men wear badges," she observed. "You're lawmen?"

"Yes," James said flatly. He could see where this conversation was going to lead and somehow thought things were going to get a little tense around the camp when it got there.

"You hunting somebody?" Rachel asked.

"Yup," from James.

"A desperado, I suppose." She wouldn't let it drop.

"Supposed to have killed a man," James said. "A judge's brother, no less."

Davey sat there, unmoving. His gun was buried under layers of coat. Somehow he didn't feel threatened by these four men, anyway. Least not while they were guests in his own camp.

"You figure this killer is close?" Rachel wanted to know. This was sounding exciting.

"Pretty close, ma'am," James said. He and Watt looked at each other, both expressionless.

"Well, that certainly is exciting," Rachel said. "Imagine, a desperate outlaw out here somewhere! I feel safe, though, with all you men here to protect me."

James favored her with a wry smile.

"Tell me," she said. "What is his name? Maybe I've heard about him."

"I believe you have heard about him, ma'am," James said in the same flat tone, "on account of you're sitting right next to him."

Rachel looked at him blankly for a long moment; then the idea thundered home, and she gasped and looked up at Davey, shocked. He said nothing; there was nothing he could say. He just watched her as she tried to take it all in.

Rachel was never more surprised in her life. When Mom had died, she had been stunned; when Paw had beat her the first time, she had been crushed and full of pain;

when Alvin had grabbed at her and held her with deadly serious intent, she had been afraid, but they all paled in front of this. Never had she been so shocked by a sudden turn of events.

And yet, somewhere deep inside, part of her stayed calm and sound thinking. This part of her rejected any notion that this man, this savior of hers, could have possibly done anything as heinous as murder. She knew him. She had lived with him. To even think her Davey might be someone of low character was not possible, and it was obvious that these men were making a big mistake.

She jumped to her feet. "Get out of here," she said to the four men, and all were amazed at the hard hatred in her voice. Davey's mouth actually dropped open in surprise. "I want you out of our camp, and I want you out of here now." Her voice left no doubt she meant every word. "The very idea that you're after a man who saved your miserable lives and welcomed you into his camp is disgusting."

She was a she-bear protecting her young—no, a full-grown woman protecting her man. "If there is anyone of low moral character around this fire, I don't think it's

Davey or me. Get on your horses and get
out." She turned away from them. "If it had
been up to me," she said, her back to them,
"I would have left you out in the storm!"

There was a moment of stunned silence
as the shocked men took it all in and
thought on it. Davey had never been more
impressed by a woman in his whole life.
Everything he had ever heard about women
paled before the sight of Rachel standing up
to four men in his favor. She had never
asked him if he was guilty or innocent; she
had just known. She trusted him. No matter
how long he lived, no matter what Rachel
would do from now on, as far as he was
concerned this would be her finest moment.

"Now, hold on, Miss Rachel," Rubin said.
"In case you ain't noticed, we have not taken
this desperado into custody. Fact is, we have
not even considered it."

Rachel turned back and looked at him.
Her hands were balled into tight little fists.

"You can unwind just a little, ma'am,"
Rubin went on. "We are not going to do
nothing to him, at least not just now. We
understand about him saving our lives and
taking us into his own camp, and while
them other three men may be rotten and

despicable, I cannot find it in my own self to take advantage of such a situation."

"What do you mean, we're rotten and despicable?" James asked in feigned anger. "Why don't you ever say nothing nice about us?"

"I will, I will," Rubin promised. "Soon as I can come up with something that don't sound too much like a lie."

Wyatt looked up at Rachel as she stood there unchanged. Her little fists were tight clenched, and he admired the spunk of this little girl/woman ready to fight for her man. He almost smiled as he looked at the amazed expression on Watt's face.

"Ma'am," he said, "you can rest easy. We got no plans to arrest Watt right now. Fact is, we're grateful to him, and besides, we was talking and think he's getting an unfair deal on account of the man he shot was the judge's brother. Also, ma'am, we're not going to arrest him on account of I sure would not want to have to fight you for him." Wyatt leaned back, speech over.

Rachel colored, unsure whether he was making fun of her or not.

"First time I ever heard you make a joke," Rubin said to Wyatt.

"Wasn't joking," Wyatt said right back,

serious. "Rather chase a real desperado any day. Woman defending her man don't have no rules. Most dangerous thing alive to my way of thinking."

"Awww, g'wan with you," Rubin said, still not sure if Wyatt was making fun or not.

"Think about it," Wyatt answered. "How'd you like to eat her cooking if you had Watt there tied up under arrest? How safe would you feel going to sleep?"

Rubin thought that over but said nothing.

Rachel had visibly relaxed. These men could see that Davey was her man. They could see it without being told. She looked at Davey, noticing the shocked expression on his face, and became afraid of what he might say, afraid he would deny there was a relationship between them.

In a way it was a golden opportunity for her to find out if he had the same feelings for her. All she had to do was keep silent. If he didn't deny she was his woman, why— she *was* his woman. The thought startled her. It was the first time she had really allowed herself to think there might be something there, something they could build on, something they could make steady and fine. It was the first time she ever really allowed herself to imagine that Waldo would not be the end, but might rather be a beginning.

All she had to do was keep silent. If Davey didn't speak . . . if Davey didn't speak. . . . Davey looked like he was about to say something, and she felt the frantic fear inside.

"How did Davey kill that man?" Rachel asked.

Davey settled back, and for at least a little while longer she was safe. He could still be *her* man, least until he said different. Somehow it didn't seem fair, though. Not fair for her to have her feelings all laid bare like that when his were still such a dark mystery.

"Watt here was born under a dark star, seems like," James answered. "It's like trouble dogs his trail no matter where he goes. He's tolerable fast with that gun of his, and people are always forcing him to prove it— people like the judge's brother who had heard about Watt's reputation and was trying to make a name for himself. Even people who don't know him seem to feel obliged to egg him on and back him into a corner where he has to protect himself."

Rachel thought that over. It didn't sound so bad, after all. Davey had merely been defending himself, according to these men, and they were lawmen and should know. Maybe if he had a good woman and settled down somewhere....

"Like that miner in Waldo the other day," Rubin said. "For no other reason than to show off in front of his drunk friends, he backed Watt there into a corner, insulted him real bad, and finally, when Watt still didn't do nothing, he drew down on him and forced Watt to take his pistol to hand and shoot him dead."

"Self-defense, sure enough," Greg said. "Fact is, Watt waited a lot longer to shoot him than I would have."

"They're right," Wyatt said. "People seem to take a fast dislike to Watt there, for no apparent reason. Don't really know why on account of I always kinda liked him myself. Besides, to my way of thinking, taking a dislike to him has not proved to be real healthy in the past."

Rubin snorted a laugh. "For that man Wagner in Waldo, it was the biggest and last mistake he ever made. Come to think of it, it proved to be the biggest and last mistake any of them ever made."

Rachel was starting to feel better. Davey couldn't help defending himself. It was a man's right to protect himself from the stupid in the land. Suddenly she actually heard what Rubin had said and stopped breathing.

"What was his name?" she asked.

Davey looked at her, concerned. She dropped to a rock like her legs couldn't hold her up anymore, and her face had gone suddenly white as a ghost.

"Whose name?" Rubin asked.

"The man in Waldo," she said flatly.

"I believe it was Wagner, ma'am," Rubin said. "Don't know his Christian name, but he was stocky, with a frequent busted nose. You know him, do you?"

The question hung there in a silence that dragged out. The five men looked at the young woman, concerned. She looked awful all of a sudden, like she had aged ten years before their eyes.

"Davey," she finally said, and her voice was full of pain and hurt. "Davey. My God! You shot my paw!"

The first man took the slug deep in his right side, and it flung him back into the man behind. His eyes were open wide with the surprise of it all. The third man in line was surprised, too. He wasted no time in going for his gun, but it was under his coat, and he only got the one button ripped open when Glen's second shot took him fair in the neck and he fell backward into the man behind and slid down to the floor.

Glen's teeth were gritted tight in hate, and he thumbed back the hammer and aimed into the frantic cluster of men trying to get back out the door. His forty-five bucked in his fist, and the slug went somewhere into the milling mass of men. Again and again his gun slammed lead into them, and then it was empty, and he flipped open the gate to reload. Jefferson's moment of stunned shock ended as he saw one of the men aim a pistol in his direction, and he went from surprise to shooting all at once.

The barroom was filled with yelling men and the booming of Jefferson's forty-five. Then some of McKnote's men managed to get their weapons unlimbered, and shots rang out from both ends of the barroom.

Steve dropped behind his bar, shocked at the speed with which gunfire had erupted. The sound of shots was almost continuous, explosions so loud in the enclosed space, they hurt his ears. Stinging smoke and the smell of cordite drifted down where he lay huddled on the floor. He heard a man grunt hard as a heavy lead slug smashed into him. Another slug crashed into the bottles on the back bar, and some of his expensive whiskey dripped to the floor like rain. Steve could smell whiskey and the copper smell of fresh blood. He huddled lower behind his walkway and wished for the violence to end.

It seemed to go on for a long time, but really was over in less than three minutes. The other corner of the room grew quiet, and four final, measured shots blasted out from by the door, then silence once more. Steve gingerly got to his feet and stepped up on the walkway to survey the damage. He slowly raised his head over the bar. McKnote came slamming through the door, gun in hand. He was puffing hard from his run up the street in the snow.

The place looked like a slaughterhouse. Men were down all around the door, some clutching themselves and moving rhythmically in their agony, some lying still and staring sightlessly. The lucky ones were standing motionless, shocked to the very core of their being. Their guns hung listlessly at their sides until, one by one, they put them back in their holsters like machines. Blood was everywhere, staining the floor in great sheets of crimson and sprayed in spotted dots here and there on the bar and tables where smashing bullets had blasted it from the bodies of living men.

Across the room was another area of carnage and death. One man was sitting on the floor, leaning forward in an unnatural position. A smear of red on the wall behind him told where he had been standing when the bullets that ended his life slammed him against the wall. He was sitting in a pool of his life's blood, but it was obvious he wasn't using it anymore.

The other one was also sitting, leaning up against an overturned table. His front was marked with red in five different places, small blossoms showing where hot lead had violated his body. Not yet dead, he glared across the room at the survivors, his still-smoking gun held loosely in his useless hand.

McKnote was in shock. Never before had he witnessed such carnage, and the men who were down had worked for him, were well known to him. They were his friends. Gun hanging at his side, he walked across the room, shuffling like an old man. He looked down at the man who was glaring up at him.

"Why?" he asked in a voice that didn't even sound like his own.

The man's eyes glowed cold and hard, hatred plain. "You hung Markie," he said, plain as day. He took in another breath, and McKnote could easily hear the awful gurgling from the blood in the man's throat. "Damn you, McKnote," he said, and blood leaked from his mouth and ran down his chin. Another awful gurgling breath. "Damn you and all of your men too."

So it was all his fault, after all. All because he had hung that boy by mistake. The man's eyes held his, locked in a transfer of hate. The pain in McKnote went deep. All his fault. Just because he had wanted to prove something to his men, wanted to show them he was still tough, still a man to be reckoned with.

But the boy had been innocent.

He hadn't been quite right in the head, either. More like a small boy in an almost man's body. He had been terrified and obviously didn't understand what was happening or why. He had cried. Not like a man at all. More like a small child. Cried like his heart was breaking, only McKnote hadn't cared then. Hadn't cared because he was trying to be the McKnote of old. But the McKnote of old was gone forever, and now the poor kid was gone forever. And he had not been guilty at all.

Sometimes, when he closed his eyes and tried, McKnote could see the kid sitting on the horse, rope around his neck. His eyes had been so scared. He had pleaded with them, but they hadn't paid him any heed, and his eyes had been so scared. And McKnote himself had quirted the horse, and the kid had squealed an awful squeal that was cut off hard as the rope jerked tight and the world came to an end for the kid as he swung squirming at the end of a twisted rope.

And he had been innocent. He had been somebody's child who had been loved and cared for. And McKnote had killed him without mercy.

He looked into the hate-filled eyes and understood. It was his fault. His fault, only his men were paying for it too.

He recognized the man. He was the one who had showed up right after they hung the kid. He had showed up and gone wild and started shooting, only Rocky had brought him down with a lucky shot. And now he had gone wild again, but this time McKnote's men hadn't fared so well. Mc-Knote stared into the evil eyes and suddenly realized the man was glaring at him from beyond the grave. He was dead. But if hatred could exist by itself, it would surround McKnote for as long as he lived. Maybe longer. He felt old. Old and guilty.

He turned away from the eyes he would never forget and went to see to his men.

Whip and Roger and Mark and David and Peter and Simon were dead. Six men. Men he knew. Men with families who were depending on McKnote to take care of their men, only he hadn't. Not this time.

Eighteen children were now without fathers. Six women were widows. It was all his fault. The weight of them rounded his shoulders. He hadn't known a man could be so tired.

Ralph was wounded bad and was carried back to one of the rooms. At least he was single. Good man, though. Two others were hurt, only not real bad. All in all, a rotten morning.

Steve was seeing to the cleanup. Now that it was over, he was excited. What a battle! His place would be famous. People would come by from all around just to see the place where such a magnificent fight had occurred. And they would drink.

He had the bodies carried down to Jebb's

stable. Jebb would make coffins for them. That would keep him busy for a while. Lot of money to be made in a town by people dying. Steve was really sorry there wasn't a photographer around. Man could make a lot of money with pictures of eight bodies lined up in a row. He could have maybe even posed them with their guns in hand. He sprinkled sawdust on the pools of red that stained his floor, but he knew the stains would not go away. Good. Folks would want to see them, anyway.

Things changed around the campsite, and Watt felt the hurt and knew he had brought it on himself. It was always that way. It was the way his life unrolled.

His skill with a gun had once more brought him pain. But he couldn't see an alternative, any way to have changed the outcome in Waldo. The miner had forced Watt to kill him. It was that simple, like it had been ordained and they were both just going through the moves.

The man had been slightly drunk and just as obnoxious and stupid as he could be. It was hard to imagine that he was Rachel's father. She must have had a really wonderful mother; that was the only reason she could have turned out so good. Of course she no longer wanted anything to do with him, and it was a deep surprise how much that hurt.

Oh, she still cooked for him and poured his coffee and all, but she never looked at him. She never looked him in the eye, and he knew it was because she would never be able to do so again without seeing him as the man who killed her father with a gun. Once again, any hope he had for a decent future had been ended in that split second when his gun had leaped into his hand and his finger had squeezed the trigger. That explosion of sound, only an instant of noise and fury, changed life forever, both in front of and behind the gun. The man in front was dead, and the man behind was emptied like a vessel, emptied of the warmth of life just as surely as if he had been the loser instead of the winner.

Watt wanted to take his gun and throw it into the snowy bushes. Wanted to heave the evil thing away and change his life forever, but he didn't. The gun was only a steel tool, and throwing it away would do nothing for him. It was the man who was really the evil weapon, and he couldn't throw himself away as much as he would like to.

He looked across the fire at the young woman where she sat huddled in his dust coat. The fire flickered red highlights from her face, and her downcast eyes mirrored the pain he felt inside. She didn't look back at him. Rubin had offered her his spare blanket, as had James, and she had made herself a bedroll halfway around the fire from him. It was like she was still there but gone forever, and he would be empty somehow until the day he died. It was a long night for them both, and they both slept colder than they had the night before.

Morning broke with only scattered clouds marring the red of the morning sky to remind them of the storm that had changed their lives. Before breakfast was over, snow began to slide from the heavy-laden bushes, and drops of icy water filtered down through the trees as the white stuff melted.

"Be able to get out of here tomorrow," Greg observed. "Make it to Waldo by evening if the mud isn't too bad."

Watt finished his coffee and rose to his feet. "I'll go get us something to eat for tonight," he announced and, taking his rifle to hand, he walked off into the woods. Rachel watched him go, then poured herself the last of the coffee and sat down where he had been sitting.

"You are a good cook, ma'am," Rubin said across the fire.

"Thank you," she answered in a listless, flat tone. "I learned by taking care of my paw."

Rubin looked across at her until she was forced to raise her eyes to his.

"Your paw didn't give him no choice," Rubin said. "No choice at all. He was drinking and showing off, and he pulled his gun on the wrong man, and that's the way of it. Watt had to kill him or be killed. It was that simple. Any one of us here would have done the same thing."

Rachel looked dully at him. "It doesn't sound like Paw at all," she said. "He had a temper, sure enough, but he always respected other men and asked for nothing more than to be left alone."

"Whiskey sometimes brings out the worst in a man," Wyatt observed.

"Even if that's so," Rachel came back, "it does not change a thing. Davey is the man who killed my paw. Shot him down to the floor in a dirty barroom."

"You must understand," Rubin said, "he

couldn't help any of it. He was just in the wrong place at the wrong time."

"I think I can understand," Rachel said. "Only, I can't forget. I'll never be able to forget." And that was the bad of it. No matter how much she loved Davey and no matter how much he loved her, if he loved her at all, life could never work out between them. Her paw would always be there, hanging between them, an unseen accusation holding them apart.

In the woods, Watt watched a small doe pawing at the snow, trying to reach the grass below. He could have shot her long ago and had meat enough for dinner, only he had not been in any hurry. Once he killed dinner, there would be no reason to remain away from the camp, away from the accusing eyes of the girl/woman who was tormenting him so.

His inadvertent sigh brought the doe's head up, and she stared straight at him for a long, motionless moment before she dismissed him and returned to her foraging. Davey looked down his sights at the small animal but didn't pull the trigger. He was so tired of killing things. It didn't seem right that always something else had to die just so he could stay alive. Now it was the deer, an inoffensive animal that just happened to be in the wrong place at the wrong time. Before, it had been the man, courage and stupidity both buoyed by alcohol.

The rifle crashed and slammed back into his shoulder. The deer went down, kicked twice, and was still. He walked over to examine his handiwork. It was a good, clean kill. He was very good at that.

Chapter Six

The snow had melted all day and all night, the temperature remaining well above the freezing mark, and morning found them mounting up for the ride to Waldo. Now there were six where there had only been two before. Rachel took Watt's hand and swung up behind just like before, only it was not the same, and both of them knew it.

They had talked it over during breakfast and decided that the four lawmen would take turns in the lead, each bucking the snow for the others until their horses began to tire. Because Horse was already carrying double, Watt would stay in the back.

The four lawmen started out joking and

talking like always, but neither Watt nor Rachel had joined in, and soon they rode in silence broken only by the squeaking of the saddles and the slogging of the horses hooves in the wet snow. Midmorning.

"Ma'am," Watt said, so softly she almost missed it.

"Yes, Mr. Watt?" Somehow she could no longer bring herself to call the killer of her father by his first name.

Watt noticed and tried to understand. "Rachel—" He was desperately intent. It was important that she believe what he was about to say. "Rachel, he gave me no choice."

Rachel said nothing. No matter what the circumstances, Paw would always stand between Watt and her.

Watt waited for a reply. Anything. Any sign that she might be willing to listen to reason. Rachel said nothing, and they rode on to the cold sounds of the horses plodding through the wet snow. The minutes dragged out. Watt could feel her back there. She was actually leaning against him, but it had nothing to do with her wanting to be close to him, and he knew it. This day's ride would end with them in Waldo, and Rachel would slide down from Horse, and that would be the last time he would ever be so close to her.

"I'm truly sorry, Rachel," he finally said, and even he wasn't sure what it was he was feeling sorriest about. Horse plodded on.

"I understand, Mr. Watt," Rachel finally said. She didn't really understand. She had practically told everyone that she was in love with him when she had attacked the other four back at the camp. Davey—Mr. Watt had said nothing in kind. She believed he liked her, maybe even loved her, but she couldn't be sure.

Of course it really wouldn't matter, what with Paw lying underground because of Davey—Mr. Watt—but she would like to know. It would be something she could think back on and wonder about as the days passed and she grew older. Something that would make her mind easier, like having a place to hide when things started to bear down on her especially hard.

For now, she had to think on practical things, like what she was going to do without Paw to take care of her. Or Mr. Watt. Even now he was right there, so solid and secure, right in front of her. But he might as well be a million miles away. Nope—she was on her own and would be on her own from now on.

The world felt empty.

Most likely Paw hadn't left much of an estate. Maybe just a few dollars, maybe nothing at all. For sure she couldn't go back to where Alvin had the wagon, because if he wasn't dead, he would be furious, and Alvin was scary enough when he wasn't angry. Of course, he might be dead, and then she could claim Paw's wagon and stuff, but she didn't think a little scalding would be enough to do Alvin in. In fact, he might even be looking for her, looking to finish what he started what seemed like so long ago.

In a way, she hoped that if Alvin was looking for her, he would find her before Mr. Watt had gone. Davey wouldn't let anyone hurt her while he was around; she knew that for sure. She thought on that for a while.

He really would *not* let anyone hurt her. She knew it somehow. He wouldn't even think about it, just act in that certain way of his, and maybe that told her enough about what she wanted to know. Maybe that was as close to love as Davey Watt could come. Maybe he did love her, only couldn't find the words to say it. Maybe. On the other hand, he probably wouldn't let anyone hurt a lost puppy, either. Nope. Until he said something, she just couldn't be sure. Not that it mattered.

Horse plodded on, and the two people moved together to his motion like one.

Come noon the sun was bright in the sky, and here and there patches of ground began to show through the snow. Greg happened to be in the lead at the time, and he reined in to a halt. The others gathered around.

"I don't see no likelihood of having a fire," he said, "so I guess we'll just keep on keepin' on if it's all the same to the rest of you. We can eat some jerky and take a five-minute rest stop here."

Rubin swung down and stretched. "Well, if you ain't the biggest sissy I have ever seen," he said to Greg. "Seems like we hardly got started, and right away you want to take a rest stop."

"I was thinkin' about the lady," Greg said, "and besides, it don't seem like you wasted any time gettin' out of the saddle yourself."

"Felt it was my duty to help the lady dismount," Rubin said, and he reached up to help Rachel down.

"Sure," came back in a tone that left no doubt he didn't believe Rubin at all.

James began handing big pieces of jerky around. "Here," he said to Rubin. "You still have enough teeth left to chew on this?"

Of course, Rubin took offense right away. "What do you mean?" he said and grabbed the jerky from James's hand. "I got all my teeth yet." He bared them in an exaggerated grin. "In fact, you're older than me," he finished his tirade.

"I didn't figure you lost your teeth on account of age," James came back real calm. "I figured you lost them on account of your bad attitude."

Rubin rolled his eyes. "Bad attitude?" He sounded shocked. "Me?"

"No offense," James said.

"Too late," Rubin put in. "The only one with a bad attitude here is you, not me. I have been brave, helpful, cheerful, thrifty, reverent, and kind right from the start."

James snorted, but before he could continue the argument, Greg butted in.

"I hate when you guys do that," he complained. "You drivel on until you make a man feel tired all the way through. Day in and day out. Drivel, drivel, drivel."

"Drivel?" Rubin asked. "What do you mean drivel? We don't say nothing unless it's truly important, and if you don't believe me, we can ask old Wyatt there."

The three turned to Wyatt, who looked back and gave an exaggerated sigh of disgust.

"If'n you don't shut up for once, me'n Watt will be forced to take our guns to hand and shoot you all," he said with an exaggerated drawl. "Man deserves a little peace and quiet now and again."

Rubin grinned and swung back aboard. He kicked his horse into motion, and they were off once more.

"Violence," he called back over his shoulder. "I am threatened with violence from one of my own partners. What is this world coming to?"

His friends grinned at his back. The grins didn't last too long as the melted snow turned the earth to mud beneath their hooves.

The sun hung red and low, seemed like right in their faces, as they single-filed into Waldo. Six mud-splattered, tired people on five exhausted horses. They slow-walked up to the stable and reined in.

Jebb opened the door. He knew right away who they were. As if there hadn't been enough killing in his quiet little town.

'Course, it looked like the lawmen had Watt under arrest, so maybe things would stay calm.

"Howdy," he said. The woman was mounted behind Watt. She was all wrapped up, but as much of her face as Jebb could see looked right pleasant. They dismounted as he gave his little speech.

"Horses are twenty-five cents a night . . ." and so forth. He could hear McKnote's men moving around behind him, talking softly among themselves. They didn't know the man they had come so far to kill was just outside the door. 'Course, if he was under arrest, they couldn't very well do anything, anyway. Jebb swung the door wide and stepped aside. The lawmen and Watt led their horses inside, and the door closed behind them.

As their eyes adjusted to the dark inside the barn, the men became aware of the crowded conditions and studied on the passel of men in various positions of rest throughout the barn. They appeared to present no threat. Just a bunch of cowhands sleeping out the storm. Funny they hadn't moved on, though.

"Howdy," Rubin said and nodded at the men. He led his horse to the center of the barn and stripped the saddle. The others followed suit.

McKnote was watching from the corner, eyes bright. He knew who they were. Watt was the tall one, and the others must be the lawmen they had heard about. He was relieved. Watt was apparently in custody. That meant no more of his men would die. No more killing. No more being killed.

Watt's two brothers were boxed up out back along with six of his own men, all waiting for burying tomorrow. They would all be put in the same ground together, the good and the bad, although even McKnote wasn't sure which was which when it came right down to it.

Were the Watt men bad for wanting to avenge their kin? He thought not. Were his men bad for carrying out his orders and dying because of it? Didn't seem like it.

Seemed like there was only one bad man in town, and that was himself. His orders had brought all this pain and suffering on all the different families. The Watts felt the pain. His men's families were going to feel the pain. And McKnote? He felt some of the pain too. Some of the pain and a whole lot of guilt. But mostly he just felt old. Nobody had ever been as old as he felt.

He watched as the six people walked out, heading for the hotel and a cooked meal, probably. There they would find out about the gun battle of this morning. Watt would find out that his family was even smaller than he had first thought. McKnote closed his eyes and slowly lay back on the straw. Weariness washed through him. More pain coming for Watt. More reason for hate. Would it never end?

He was glad the lawmen had Watt. Maybe it would be over now.

Steve watched the six of them come into his bar. Five men and a woman. He recognized Watt and the four lawmen. They came in through the door and walked right over the bloodstains on the floor. They immediately began to peel off their coats to soak up some of the heat from the stove.

He was dumbstruck when he saw that Watt still had his gun. He wasn't under arrest, after all. He felt the sense of danger tingle on the back of his neck. Watt wasn't going to like it when he found out what had happened here. Maybe there was more history about to happen in his place.

The heat hit Watt as he walked in. It had been so long since he had felt warm. His

fingers felt thick and useless as they fumbled with the buttons on his coats. He hung
them on one of the pegs along the back wall
and sat down, back to the corner. It was the
very seat his brother Jefferson had sat in
less than ten hours before but, of course, he
didn't know that. Watt looked at the bullet
holes in the table with amusement. He remembered this place had come to life with
miners after sundown, and it looked like
they had been at it again.

The lawmen dragged up chairs and joined
him. The woman sat in the middle of the
four lawmen, her back to the door. There
was something wrong with her dress, like
it had been torn and then sewed back together.

Steve went over to take their order.
"What'll it be?" he asked.

Rubin indicated the holes in the table.
"Boys get a little wild, did they?" he asked
in good spirits.

"Something like that," Steve answered
carefully. He studied the woman without
appearing to.

She was a young thing, although the
trials of the last few days had left her eyes
looking older than her face. Her hair could
use some work on account of it was tangled

and knotted, but on the whole she was a pretty young thing. 'Course, women had no business in a bar.

"Steak for everybody," Rubin said. "Bring five beers and a glass of milk for the lady."

"Would the lady like to eat in the back?" Steve asked, leaving no doubt as to what he thought about women in bars.

"She'll stay with us," Rubin said, and his tone left no doubt that Steve should not mention it again.

So this is a bar? Rachel was thinking. She had never been in one before. In fact, she didn't know a girl or woman who had. It didn't seem as evil as she had been led to believe by Paw. In fact, it seemed rather plain, sort of like a restaurant except for the long bar down one side. A door by the open end of the bar probably led back to the kitchen, since that was where the bartender had gone after taking their order. Another door next to that one led back to the rooms. She felt uncomfortable a little, made that way by the obvious feelings of the bartender that she didn't belong, but when she looked at the five men around her, she no longer worried.

"Feel a little strange?" Rubin asked.

She nodded. "A little," she admitted.

"Why don't they want women to come in here?"

"It's for their own protection," Wyatt replied before anyone else could. "These places don't always attract the best of men, and when they get a little red-eye in them, a decent woman wouldn't care to be around."

"I see," and Rachel did see. After all, look what happened with Alvin when he got a little drunk.

"Nobody's gonna bother you," Greg said flat and plain.

"I'm not worried while you men are here," Rachel assured them.

Steve came over and put the five beers down in front of the men, then carefully set a glass of milk in front of Rachel.

"Few of the miners will probably be coming in soon," he said.

"You had best tell them to mind their manners while there's a lady present," Rubin advised.

"I'll do that," Steve said. He had already planned on that.

Dinner was tolerable, especially after range food for so long, although there wasn't a whole lot of conversation. Rachel couldn't help feeling she was at a crossroads in her life, like she was at the end of something or the beginning of something else. She wanted to keep looking at Davey, but for some reason kept her eyes on her plate.

Steve cleared the plates, then came back over with the coffeepot when the door burst open and half a dozen miners walked in.

"Whooee!" the first said. "Look at all the blood," and they studied the big stain by the door.

"More over in the corner, I'm thinking," another said, and they looked across the room at the corner, for the first time realizing there were people back there.

"Howdy," the first said. "We just come in to have a drink and see where all the shooting happened."

Steve started back toward the bar.

"Hold it a minute," Rubin said, and Steve walked back, face expressionless.

"You had some shooting here?" Rubin asked.

"Yup."

"Why didn't you tell us about it? We're the law, you know."

"Didn't care to tell of it in front of the lady," Steve said.

"She's a tough one," Rubin told him. "She can take it. Somebody get killed in here?"

"Yup." Steve wasn't real anxious to get into this.

Rubin was beginning to get annoyed. "So tell us about it," he ordered in his hard lawman voice. "Who was killed and how?"

"There were eight killed all told," Steve said in a resigned voice. That sure got their attention.

"Eight?" James was amazed.

They all were amazed; that was clear enough by their expressions. Steve couldn't see the woman's face from where he was, though.

"Yup," Steve came back. "Six over by the door and two here where you're sitting." To a man they all looked at the floor under the table, for the first time noticing the bloodstains not quite scrubbed away.

"Now that ought to make my dinner set better," James said in a sarcastic tone. "How did it happen?"

It was the question Steve really didn't want to answer, but try as he might, there didn't appear to be any way around it.

He sighed. "Two men were sitting here having breakfast this morning," he began. "These other men started coming in the door. As soon as the one who had his back to the door turned and saw them, he jumped to his feet and yelled, 'Jeff. It's them what hung Markie!' and commenced to shooting." Steve watched the startled expression flick across Watt's face, and they looked eyeball to eyeball as he finished his tale. He could easily see the blood drain from the man's face.

"I dropped behind the bar," he went on, "and when the shooting stopped, I came up and found six dead by the door, with another bad hurt and two more just winged. The two at this table were dead. Names were Glen and Jefferson Watt."

"What were the names?" Rachel asked, shocked.

"Watt, ma'am," Steve said. "They were his brothers, I'm thinking."

Watt's face had gone completely pale, eyes shocked. It took a hard moment for it to sink in and become real.

Glen and Jeff, dead. They died right where he was sitting, and that red stain on the floor was Watt blood that had been pulsing through his brothers even this morning.

He could almost see it happen in his mind. Glen had always been a little rash and impulsive. He had seen the men, recognized them, and started in to shooting. Poor Jefferson, always a thoughtful and quiet man, had probably been surprised to his very bottom. He, too, would have started shooting when he saw there was no other way to defend himself or his brother. He was a rancher, not a shootist, but he was strong and hard and would have stood there and traded shots until they blew the life from him and put him down for good.

Watt had never seen a gunfight of such proportions, but he had seen a lot of gunfights and could easily see in his mind how it had been. The crashing of guns in a closed room, the smell of gunsmoke, and probably men screaming in fear and pain. His brothers relentlessly triggering off rounds from right there, two indistinct forms sending streaks of fire through the smoke surrounding them like fog. A few minutes of noise and fear and yells and then red hurt as McKnote's men got some of their own bullets home. Then quiet once more except for the moaning of hurt and dying men. The place would have smelled of gunpowder and blood. Some of it Watt blood. His brothers' blood.

Watt opened his mouth to speak, but nothing came out. He noticed the tears glistening in Rachel's eyes. Now why would she be crying? He took a sip of beer and tried again.

"McKnote?" he asked. "Did he survive?" His expressionless voice was terrible to hear.

"He did," Steve answered. "By the time he got here, it was all over. He looked around like he was in a daze, then went over to your brother Glen and was with him when he died. Glen said something to him, but we couldn't hear."

Watt took it in. He could almost imagine what Glen would want to say to McKnote. His chair scraped on the floor as he started to get to his feet.

"Hold it, Watt!" Rubin said, hard and loud.

Watt stopped and looked down at him.

"There's been enough killing already," Rubin went on.

Watt nodded. "I know," he said soft and low, almost sad. "But this is something I got to do." He hesitated, then, "This man has gone and killed three of my family. What would you do?"

Rubin sat back in his chair and thought on that for a second. "Well, I surely wouldn't go charging in without knowing what the picture was," he said. "Shooting first and figuring later seems likely to be the reason your brothers are dead right now. You don't know how many of them there are, how they're feeling, or even if McKnote is still in town. Now sit and think. You're wore out clean through already. A good night's rest maybe will help you think on this clearly in the morning."

Watt passed his hand in front of his eyes. Rubin was right. He was tired, tired clear through to the bone.

"Davey," Rachel said, quiet desperation in her tone. He looked down at her, and she was shocked at the hard empty in his eyes before she realized it was meant for Mc- Knote, not her. "Listen to him, Davey," she implored. "Just sleep on it. One more night can't make that much difference."

He held her eyes for a long moment, then dropped to his seat, almost relieved.

"All right," he said. "I'll sleep on it." And then, sarcastically, "A man should do his killing when he's well rested."

Morning came gentle and easy, and the soft breeze held out the promise of Indian summer. Snow was melting, and mud was everywhere, would be everywhere for days. The sound of hammering from the stable told of Jebb finishing up coffins for the eight men who had passed from the land of the living. Steve carried out the tray of breakfast for the man who would probably add to that total.

"Here you are, Mr. Watt," he said as he set the plate of bacon and eggs and potatoes down. Watt didn't look so good this morning, but then Steve expected he wouldn't have slept well, either, had he been in Watt's place. Must be hard to all of a sudden find out your family has been cut down all at once.

Watt reached for his fork; then his hand changed direction and darted down to his gun as the front door suddenly opened.

Rubin grinned over at Watt and closed the door behind him. "Morning," he said.

"Morning," Watt acknowledged as the tension ran out of him and he reached for his fork once more. He began shoveling in the food as Rubin sat down across from him.

Steve brought another cup of coffee for Rubin and then went back to his bar. He was grateful for the hard oak front on the bar. It had been expensive but had proved its worth yesterday when the slugs were flying. Looked like he might have to shield himself behind it again today, the way things were developing. Yes, sir, his place was definitely going to be famous. Steve just hoped he wouldn't be too dead to enjoy it.

"I just seen McKnote," Rubin said as he sipped at the hot brew. Watt stopped chewing and looked across at him. His eyes were flat, expressionless, hard.

"How many of them are there?" he asked.

"Nine of them, looks like," Rubin responded. "One of them is hurt bad, and two of them are slightly shot. I'd say you're looking at going up against eight men."

Watt looked at him for a moment, grunted, and resumed eating.

Rubin watched for a moment. "Another thing," he went on. "They strike me as pretty loyal to McKnote. Seems like you'll have to go through all seven before you ever get to the man you're after." He leaned back. "You know, a man can't be all bad if he can get all those men to show that kind of loyalty. Maybe he just made a mistake. All men make mistakes now and again. Even you."

Watt said nothing, kept eating, but Rubin knew he was thinking. He let him mull it over for a few minutes.

"Listen, Watt," he said when he thought the time was right, "he wants to talk to you." That stopped the chewing. "I think you ought to at least talk to the man," Rubin went on. "Can't hurt nothing, and maybe some good will come of it."

Watt leaned back in his chair and studied Rubin. "The man hung a backwards boy," he said. "Poor Markie never did anything to hurt a living soul. McKnote hung him for stealing livestock. The man hung an innocent, slow-witted child," he repeated. "There can be no excuse for that and no excusing it, either." He sipped at his coffee. "I'll talk to him, though," he said. "I would like to see just what kind of man can do such a thing before I kill him."

"So you'll talk to him. No trouble?" Rubin asked.

Watt shook his head. "No trouble 'less he starts it," he said.

Rubin pushed back his chair. "I'll go get him," and he went out.

Steve took the opportunity to refill Watt's cup, then went back to the bar but stayed down at that end. Might be interesting to listen.

The woman walked into the bar from the back. She looked over at Watt, unsure if she should join him. Watt looked at her for a moment, then pointedly looked away.

Steve hurried over to her. "Morning, ma'am," he said. She nodded. "Be happy to serve you your breakfast in your room," he offered.

Rachel looked at Watt, wanting him to turn and smile and invite her to sit down. Watt studied his coffee.

Rachel sighed. "My room will be fine," she said. Two men in her life, and she had lost them both. Lost them both with the same shot. It wasn't fair. She turned and went back down the hall.

The front door opened, and Rubin came in with McKnote behind. Watt studied the man he was going to kill.

McKnote's hair ringed gray around his bald pate. A small belly pushed out over his belt. He didn't look evil. He looked like the middle-aged rancher he was. They came over and sat down. His eyes were gray, too, and they showed the deep weariness of the man.

"Mr. Watt," he said softly. "This killing must stop. It's for you and I to either continue the violence or end it. I want to end it."

Watt's eyes held his, reminding McKnote of the dying man from yesterday, but McKnote went on.

"I'm tired, Mr. Watt. I'm not a young man anymore, and I have made many mistakes in my life. None of them has been so horrible as what I did to young Markie Watt. I see that boy's face many times a day. I hear his pleas every day. I shall never be free of him until the day I die. I don't want to kill anymore—or be killed, either."

"I agreed to meet with you for two reasons," Watt said. "Number one, I wanted to see what kind of man it took to hang a slow-minded boy. Now I have seen, and frankly, I don't think you're too much of a man."

McKnote didn't even react to the insult.

"Number two," he went on, "I wanted to give you a chance to save the lives of the rest of your men. It's my intention to kill you, McKnote. If I have to kill seven or eight of your men to do that, I will. I wouldn't like it, but I would do it. I think it would be far better for you to meet me in the street, stand up on your own two legs like a man, and fight me fair."

McKnote gave a sad little smile. "I don't think it would be really a fair fight, Mr. Watt," he said softly. "I've heard about your prowess with a gun."

"It's as fair a chance as you're likely to

get," Watt said. "It's a whole lot better chance than you gave Markie."

McKnote flinched at that.

"What will it be, McKnote?" Watt's voice was unyielding, hard. "Are you going to get seven or eight more of your men killed, or has your life come too high already?"

McKnote's shoulders slumped, and he sighed. He thought about Rosalie and knew that he would never again see her face or feel her soft hands in his.

"Enough of my men have already paid for my stupidity," he said softly. "Their families haven't even begun to suffer yet." He sighed. "I'll meet you alone whenever and wherever you say." His voice was dejected. He thought he was almost already dead, and he thought of the six men who died because of him the day before. At least he would be in good company.

"Noon," Watt pronounced the sentence. "The sun won't be in anyone's eyes, and it will be as fair as it can be."

"Noon it is," McKnote said softly. He rose to leave.

"I would practice some if I were you," Watt said to his back.

McKnote gave a funny little laugh, but his voice was firm when he replied. "Certainly, Mr. Watt," he said. "I don't intend to make it too easy for you."

Watt watched him as he walked straight and tall to the door.

McKnote turned and looked back at him. "Until noon, Mr. Watt," he said, and then he was gone.

Chapter Seven

"So what else happened?" Rachel asked as Steve was laying out her breakfast. He was filling her in on the events that just took place in the bar.

"That's about it, ma'am," he said. "McKnote left, and they're to meet in the street at noon."

"Can Mr. McKnote beat Davey . . . Mr. Watt?"

"Not likely, ma'am."

She looked relieved. "How did Mr. McKnote take it?" she wanted to know.

Steve sighed and thought that over. "Well, ma'am," he said, "McKnote has always been a man. He lives by hard standards, and he expects others to do the same.

162

There's no give up in him. He could have easily hid behind the guns of his men, but he didn't wish to get any more of them killed. I'd say we have to be proud of McKnote."

Rachel looked troubled. "Sounds to me like he's a good man who just made an awful mistake," she said. "Are you sure he doesn't stand any chance?"

"Almost none at all," Steve confirmed. "He's a fighter, though. Always has been. He'll go down trying."

"What a waste," she said softly.

"Yes, ma'am, that it is." Steve was thinking of McKnote. Rachel was thinking of them both. He poured her coffee and headed for the door. "Now if you'll excuse me, ma'am, I have to take breakfast to the gents across the hall." Steve couldn't wait to tell them about the impending gunfight.

"Until later," Rachel said and sat down behind her table. Steve closed the door behind him.

McKnote's men had dug the holes, eight of them, side by each. The shovels had gone down through the mud into good earth, and they had worked hard and fast because McKnote wanted to see to the burying before noon.

The door opened, and a young man wearing a new sling on his left arm came in. That he was nervous was plain to see. He walked over to the corner table.

"Mr. Watt?" he asked.

"Yes." The boy/man was young, maybe seventeen or eighteen. He wasn't wearing a gun that Watt could see.

"Mr. McKnote sent me," he said. "He said I was to tell you that the holes will be dug and the burying done at eleven this morning. Said you was welcome to come and see that your brothers get buried good and proper and that you didn't have to worry none about any tricks."

Watt looked the boy/man in the eye. His brothers had probably put that young man in the sling.

"Am I supposed to believe that?" he asked.

The young man appeared startled. "Oh, I'm sure it's true," he said. "Mr. McKnote give his word."

"And McKnote is not a liar, huh?" Watt asked.

Now the boy/man looked shocked. "Oh, no, sir," he said. "Mr. McKnote always keeps his word. I ain't never heard nobody even question it before."

Watt believed him. "Okay," he said. "I'll be along."

"I'll tell him," and the young man left, his relief at the completion of his mission obvious.

Come eleven, seemed like everybody in town went to the service. Big doings in such a small town. The eight coffins were stacked side by each and one on top of another on two wagons and pulled through the mud to the smallish but fast-growing cemetery. Eight raw holes gaped open, waiting for the newly dead to take their rightful place forever.

The people walked behind, tramping through the mud, coats open to the fifty-degree warmth of the springlike day. There were McKnote's men, walking in a protective group around their boss, some of the miners, and even a few women with their husbands, mostly shopkeepers and such. The four lawmen walked together, and Watt swung in behind, slogging through mud that had already been tramped before. He looked around but didn't see Rachel and was surprised at that. Surprised and disappointed.

Some of McKnote's men, and some of the

miners lowered the coffins into the holes, carefully retrieving and coiling the ropes for the next time, which might not be too far away. McKnote looked across at Watt, and the two men locked eyes for a moment, both thinking the same thing. One of them would be lowered into a hole just like that before the sun had set tomorrow night. In spite of himself, Watt felt a shiver go down his back.

The preacher was also the keeper of the general store, and Watt had only seen him in passing. He was a short man with a bowler hat, which he removed as he waited for the men to finish up with their ropes and moving about.

"Dearly beloved," he began in an amazingly deep voice to come from such a diminutive frame. He always started all his preaching with "dearly beloved" because he liked the sound of it.

"Dearly beloved. We have come to put to rest all these men who died so fast and hard yesterday morning. Why they died, most of us ain't quite sure, but we can rest easy knowing that the Lord can doubtless sort it all out. No matter what the reason, they likely have families and friends who will grieve at their passing. We will take a moment of silence to think on these poor friends and relations."

The soft breeze blew warm in the sudden silence. Birds were crying off in the distance, and Watt realized with a shock that those boxes really did hold his brothers and they would never again please him with their presence. Sorrow hit him hard and low—sorrow at their passing, sorrow at the foolish reason for their death.

They died for nothing. Revenge. They were gone from his life forever, and it wasn't like they died for any good reason at all. Nothing could bring Markie back. And now nothing could bring Glen and Jefferson back. His life, never too full of loved ones in the first place, now had a whole lot more empty in it.

"We hope we do not ever have a tragedy like this in our town again," the preacher said. "Rest in peace in the hands of the Lord," he intoned over the graves. "Okay, boys, fill 'em up," he finished.

The men took shovels in hand, and the earth thudded back into the holes, first thumping on the boxes; then they were gone from the sight of man forever, and the holes were filled and heaped, and the people walked back to town.

Watt watched them go, men tromping straight ahead, the women dainty-stepping around the worst of the mud. They were talking among themselves, and once in a while he could even hear laughter. Their busy noise faded away, cut in sections by the slamming of doors in town as they went back to their normal lives. Soon he was alone.

The birds were singing again, and the sun was shining, and the wind was blowing soft. All these were things now forever denied Jeff and Glen. He stared at the mounds of earth, all eight of them. They were under there, killers and victims alike, much closer in death than they had ever been in life, and Watt was pretty sure the reason for their dying was not important to them anymore. Revenge, fear, hate, love, all meant nothing to them, and it was pretty clear that the only thing to be learned from all these dead men was that alive is better than dead.

Then there was Markie to be weighed into the picture. Markie with his slow ways. Markie who loved creatures and people the same. Markie who had been embarrassed and humiliated by people his whole life, yet still loved them. Markie who had been scared and picked on and tormented at the end. Markie who had probably cried and begged for more life at the end. Markie who that man in the barn down there had hung without mercy.

Now Markie and his dad and his uncle and six of the men who hung Markie were all planted under the ground, and none of it likely mattered to any of them anymore. But it still mattered to the living. Watt straightened and walked back through the mud to the hotel. It was almost noon.

The hotel bar was crowded, mostly miners who came to watch the gunfight, but the crowd parted easily in front of him, and his table in the corner was left empty. Watt went back and sat down, back to the wall. It was fifteen minutes to twelve. The rest of the people appeared to be paying him no mind, but he knew they were watching him, wondering if he was going to be dead in a few minutes. It did not seem likely.

There was a sudden commotion from down the hall, a door slamming and running feet coming toward the bar, and suddenly Rachel burst into the room. The people recoiled from her sudden entrance like a wave. She looked about frantically. Her new dress was torn down the front, and she was trying to hold it together. Blood trickled down from the corner of her mouth, and a dark bruise showed beneath her left eye.

Eyes wide with fear, she spotted Watt as he rose from the table, and he could see the fear go away and something else take its place. Satisfaction? Trust? Her expression was hard to read. She started toward him, knowing he would take care of her, but a whip snaked into the room from behind her, wrapped around her neck, and yanked her off her feet. She fell heavily to her back and lay there, stunned.

Watt's table smashed to the floor, and he was suddenly standing over her, looking at the horribly disfigured man in the hall. The man's teeth showed in a smile, but it wasn't a smile, because he had no lips. Watt knew this had to be the man she had scalded, and he could feel the hate, hot and acid, slide through his veins like never before as he looked down on Rachel gasping for air at the end of that monster's whip.

"Die!" Alvin screamed at Rachel.

She was on the floor—choking, dying slowly in front of him, and he knew the sight of her down there would keep him warm for a long time. He could see the shocked faces of people in the bar, but he knew they would not interfere. It wasn't their business and, besides, his anger and awful face would keep them away.

"Die!" he yelled again. A man stepped into the door, standing over her gasping form. Alvin opened his mouth to curse at him.

The sound of a shot coming from so close startled Watt; then he realized it was his gun that had bucked in his hand and shot fire into the hall. The monster took the slug in the belly and doubled over, wind knocked from him. Watt thumbed back the hammer, and the gun smashed another slug into the man who was killing Rachel. The whip flew from his hand, and the force of the slug made him backpedal into the hallway.

Again and again the gun spat fire and lead into the hall, each shot forcing the evil man back. Watt advanced on him with every shot until he was almost on top of the awful man and his gun was empty and the thing he had been shooting lay huddled against the end of the hall, all broken and smashed and bloody.

Rubin was coming down the hall, carrying Rachel like a doll in his arms.

"Open the door, Watt," he said and gently laid her down on the bed. He covered her with a quilt as Steve came in with a basin of water and a wet cloth. Watt found himself wiping her face with the damp cloth, willing her eyes to open.

Her eyelids fluttered several times, and then she was looking up at him.

"Hello," he said. She tried to talk, but her throat hurt, and she could only make a croaking sound. Oh. The whip. Alvin's whip.

Watt watched fear enter her eyes and shook his head.

"It's okay," he said gently. "He won't bother you again."

Rubin glanced down the hall at the crumpled figure. Truer words were never spoken. He closed the door gently, leaving the two of them alone.

Rachel felt relief flood through her. When she had seen Watt in the bar, she had known he would take care of her, that everything would be all right. She looked up at him. He looked so concerned, so worried. She felt tears flood her eyes. She wanted to talk to him, wanted to tell him how she felt, wanted to ask him how he felt, but her throat would not make any sound.

"Don't try to talk," Watt said. "Your voice will come back soon enough. Besides, I have some things I want to say, so you can just listen."

Her eyes stayed locked to his, full of tears. Why she was crying, he had no idea. Probably just glad to be alive.

"I was awful upset when I came across you out on the prairie," he began. His voice was soft and gentle, steady. Rachel knew she loved this man more than life itself.

"I was on my way to kill McKnote," he said, "and I didn't want you to hold me up." He couldn't make out her expression at all. It was almost like her eyes were smoky sort of, so intense was she looking at him.

"I think coming across you was the best thing that ever happened to me," he said, and she held her breath, waiting to hear the rest.

"I never before had anybody who needed me and yet took care of me at the same time." He smiled down at her. "Heck," he said, "I never had anybody before, period." He put his hand on her brow gently, ever so gently.

"I love you, Rachel Wagner," he said, and she closed her eyes slowly, then opened them once more. "I think," he went on, "that the two of us coulda been so much more than either of us alone." He sighed, and his eyes grew hard.

"Only, I killed the wrong man," he said. "I would take it back any way I could, but there's no way to undo an awful thing like that." He looked away from her. He couldn't bear to see the hurt in her eyes at the mention of her father. "In one second I shot away any chance we might have ever had," he went on. "Even if we was to try to forget it, we never could. Your father would always be there, always between us like a wedge in a stump."

He rose to his feet. "I will love you forever," he said. "You can rest nights and think on it, for I will be out there somewhere, and I will be thinking on it too." He walked to the door and looked back.

"Good-bye, Rachel Wagner," he said. "Now, I got something I gotta do," and he went out and closed the door softly behind him.

Rachel felt the tears flood full, then run steady down her face. She did not make any move to follow him.

"She all right?" Rubin asked Watt as he walked into the bar.

"Yup," he said. "She's gonna be fine."

Rubin looked at Watt's empty eyes and knew.

"You kinda give us a problem, you know?" he said. Watt gave him his full attention.

"You are a wanted man," Rubin went on, "and it is our job to bring you in."

Watt suddenly noticed that all four lawmen were standing there facing him.

Wyatt cleared his throat. "Warrant says 'Watt,'" he said. "I seen two graves this morning that said the same thing. I figure the Watt we wanted is one of the dead ones."

"Me too," James chimed in. "I reckon we should just go back and tell the judge that Watt is dead."

"That's pretty much the way I see it too," Greg said.

Rubin looked at Watt and sighed. "You mean you men dragged me all over this awful country after a man who turned out to be dead?" he asked.

"What do you mean we dragged you?" James said.

Rubin turned and started for the door.

"Seems like you was almighty anxious to come along with us," James went on.

The four men headed for the door like Watt wasn't there at all.

"I'm a busy man," Rubin complained. "I

don't have time to travel all over the coun-
tryside training beginners."

"Beginners!" James said. "We have forgot
more about our trade that you will ever
know!"

"Will you guys for cripes' sake shut up!"
Greg cried. "I cannot take much more of this
constant bickering. You make a man tired
clean through."

Rubin opened the door. "Bickering!" Watt
heard him say. The other men followed him
out. "I'll have you know I do not bicker!"
and the door closed and they were gone.

The moment of silence following their
leaving was suddenly broken by the wall
clock. It began chiming noon.

Watt was confused clear through. It was
like things were happening too fast for him
to keep up with. His brothers dead, the fu-
neral, the attack on Rachel, the lawmen
leaving him alone, and him telling Rachel
what he wanted to say for so long already.
Now it was noon, and he had to go out and
finally meet the man who had hung Markie
to a tree for nothing. Now it was perfectly
silent in the bar as everybody watched him
to see what he was going to do next.

He rose from the table and walked over
to the center of the bar. The crowd parted

like water in front of him. He leaned an elbow on the bar.

"Beer, please," he said softly.

Steve drew him a beer and set it in front of him. Watt sipped at the brew in silence, for all the world looking like a man who had no reason to hurry anywhere. He was just a man sipping a beer while a bar full of people watched his every move in absolute quiet.

McKnote looked back into the barn. His men were standing there in a group, watching him in silence. He had no doubt he would never see any of them again. They would be talking of him after, though, so it was important that he do what he had to do well. Wouldn't be good for Rosalie to hear he had not gone out like a man.

The breeze was warm on his face, and he could hear the birds singing with the pleasure of the warming day. He was surprised at how much he didn't want to die. Seemed like his life wasn't finished yet. There were things he had to say to his family, things he wanted to accomplish at the ranch, and there was Rosalie. So many years they had been together. How was she going to handle being all alone while she got older? He missed her already, but in a way that wasn't quite fair. His missing days were over. Hers were just about to begin, and hers would not end for a long, long time.

He sighed and turned up the street. His boots squished in the mud as he slowly walked toward the hotel. Watt was not outside yet, but McKnote had no doubt he would show up.

He stopped about halfway to the hotel and swung the side of his coat around so it was behind his gun. He loosened the heavy weapon in its leather holster.

There. He was ready. Watt hadn't showed yet, but McKnote did not mind waiting at all. Not at all.

He looked around at the blue sky, with only a puffy white cloud here and there. He saw flashes of faces looking out from behind window glass, and one of them, a small girl with eyes so serious, came into focus. She was watching, watching to see how it was when a man died. Probably her folks didn't know she was there. McKnote made himself a promise that he would be sure his shot didn't go wild, even if he was hit. He had already killed one innocent, and that was more than enough.

He would dearly love to get off a shot at

this last moment in his life. He could stand dying if he went down fighting. Darn that Watt! Where was he, anyway? Couldn't he tell when a man was ready to die?

The hotel door opened, and Watt came out. He looked casually down to where McKnote was waiting in the street, then stepped down into the mud and began to walk down toward the waiting man. Mc-Knote felt his heart speed up, begin pounding in his chest as if it knew these were the last few moments of life. He took a deep breath to steady his hands. Watt walked closer, and McKnote let his hands drop to the ready position. There. He could do no more. Now it was up to Watt. He felt sweat start to bead on his forehead.

Watt came closer, and McKnote could hear his boots squishing in the mud with each step. He was in easy pistol range, and still the man made no move toward his evil gun. McKnote wanted to draw so bad, but somehow he couldn't. He was like a bird with a snake, helpless to do anything but watch death come closer and closer. His hand trembled as it hung by his gun. Why didn't the man draw?

Watt was close, close enough for McKnote to see the bland expression on his face. How could a man be so callous that he could face the prospect of killing another man with so little emotion? How could a man appear so confident of the outcome unless he was incredibly fast? McKnote knew he was a dead man.

Watt was almost too close! And then he was too close, and he walked up to McKnote, looked away from him, and walked right on past.

"Go home, McKnote," he said softly over his shoulder, and he walked down and into the barn.

McKnote stood there trembling for a moment; then relief flooded through him, and suddenly the birds were singing again, and his eyes were flooded with tears. The man wasn't going to kill him. The man had decided that enough was enough. The man had decided to end it here and now. He saw the girl in the window and the puzzled expression on her face, and he smiled at her. After a moment she smiled back.

Watt saddled Horse in the unnatural silence of the barn. McKnote's men watched without a sound. Seemed like he was being watched by a lot of people today. It would be nice to get back out in the country, where a man had room to breathe, where life didn't happen quite so fast and confused as it did in town. He paid Jebb, waited patiently for his change, and led Horse outside. He mounted up.

McKnote was slowly walking back toward the barn, slogging through the mud. He came up to Watt, reached up and touched his hat.

"Mr. Watt," he said in passing, and then he was inside the barn, and Watt could hear his men begin to talk excitedly.

Where to go now? Seemed like he was a man without a mission. He remembered the last camp, the pretty little place buried in the trees. That was a place a man could rest up and think. That was a place a man could plan. That was a place a man could remember. He touched Horse with his heels, and they headed out of town.

Unknown to him, the four lawmen sat their horses and watched him go.

"The boy done good," Rubin declared.

"I agree," James, said.

"You agree with him?" Greg asked, surprised.

"Yes," James answered.

"Well, I'll be...." Greg said. "I never thought I'd see the day."

Wyatt booted his horse into motion and headed back toward the town.

"Hey!" Rubin called. "Where you going?"

"Celebrate," came the one-word answer.

The others knew that when Wyatt celebrated, he drank one and only one beer.

"Seems like a good idea to me," Rubin said.

"I agree," James said.

"Will you guys for cripes' sake stop agreeing with each other all the time?" Greg complained. "It's enough to make a man tired clear through." He kicked his horse into line behind the others.

A gentle knock on the door, and Steve brought Rachel's lunch tray in to her. He could see the question in her eyes and shook his head.

"Fight didn't come off," he said.

Rachel looked relieved.

"Watt walked out to meet McKnote and just walked right on by him and kept going. He got on his horse and rode out of town."

She closed her eyes for a long moment. "He didn't kill McKnote?" she croaked.

"Nope. Now there's a strange thing. McKnote seems happy enough, but every now and again he gets real serious, and you can tell he's thinking about Watt."

"He's lucky to be alive."

"I believe he's aware of that," Steve responded with a short chuckle. "He bought his men a drink to celebrate; then they took off for his ranch. I think he wanted to go home to his wife. I think Mr. McKnote is a changed man some."

"Maybe Davey is too," she said softly.

"Davey? Oh, yeah, Watt."

"Did Rubin and the others leave?" Rachel asked. Seemed like her voice was getting better as she used it.

"Yes, they did," he answered. "Only they came back after it was all over. Came back for a beer and some lunch. They're finishing up out there now. I got to get back." He rose. "Enjoy your lunch," he said and closed the door quietly behind him.

Rachel could hear Rubin laughing out in the bar. She sighed and lifted the cloth from her tray.

Swallowing had been hard and painful at first, but as she worked on her food, it got easier. Apparently Alvin's whip had done no permanent damage to her throat. She finished her glass of water and reached over to set the tray on the night table when there was a tentative knock on the door.

"Come in," she said without thinking. The door swung open.

Rubin had enjoyed his lunch. Seemed like it wasn't often they could eat inside and enjoy a beer after. But now it was time to leave. Time to head back and see what new mischief the judge had plotted out for them. He rose to his feet, and the others followed suit.

There was a loud crash of dishes falling from back of the hall, and for an instant the four men just looked at each other in surprise. Then they were running into the hall, guns at the ready. The door to Rachel's room was open.

Greg was first through the door, and before he could even say how it happened, he had the man inside against the wall, his six-gun against the stranger's throat. The man's eyes were wide with fright, but he was being very careful not to move.

"Wait!" Rachel called from where she was sitting up in the bed. "Don't shoot!"

"Hold it! Hold it!" Rubin came into the room. "Everybody just stand still and take a second here until we figure out what's what."

"Rubin!" Rachel said. "The instant I get

out of this bed, I am going to tear off your head, throw it in the corner, and call in the dogs."

That stopped them all. Rubin's eyes opened wide. "Come again?" he said.

"That man is my father! You said he was dead—and that Davey had killed him!"

Greg carefully lowered the hammer and reholstered his gun. "He don't look a whole lot dead to me," he said.

"They told me the dead man's name was Wagner," Rubin said. "They said his name was Wagner."

Rachel's father cleared his throat and rubbed his neck. "You mean Randy Wagger?" he asked. "The man who was killed in a gunfight?"

Rubin hit his forehead. "Wagger!" he said. "That's right. Wagger." He saw how the rest were looking at him. "Hey," he said, "I only got one letter wrong."

"You're a real nincompoop!" James said in disgust.

Rachel laughed, hearty and loud. "You know what this means?" she said. "Do you men know what this means?" She got out of bed, still in her torn dress. "Get out," she said. "Get out all of you! Paw, I'll be needing your horse for a while."

The four lawmen grinned down at her, then trooped from the room.

Dazed, her father followed. "I don't know what's got into her," he said as they closed the door. Rubin laughed.

Rachel looked around the room, frantic. She had nothing else to wear, nothing to ride in. She hesitated a moment, then ripped her dress up the back. She had to be able to sit a horse. She looked in the mirror. Her face was bruised under one eye, and her neck was rapidly turning black and blue. Her hair was a mess. She grinned at her image. At least he would have no trouble recognizing her.